THE GHOST OF A HORSE

Stevie shrieked as her horse gave a sideways leap and whirled, then stood with muscles trembling, ears pointing toward the fence. "What was that for?"

The other horses jumped, too. For a moment Carole felt her balance slipping. She grabbed her horse's mane and stayed on.

"Oh, no!" Lisa's voice rose high in panic. Suddenly the riders could see what had spooked their horses—a lone horse, a skinny, haggard-looking, almost-white horse, plunging toward them across four lanes of traffic!

A huge semitruck blared its horn. The horse leaped onto the grass median, ran in place for a stride, then dashed onto the other half of the highway. A passenger car slammed on its brakes, swerving around the horse. The horse raised its head and squealed desperately.

"He'll be killed!" Carole screamed.

THE SADDLE CLUB

GOLD MEDAL HORSE

BONNIE BRYANT

A SKYLARK BOOK
NEW YORK • TORONTO • LONDON • SYDNEY • AUCKLAND

Special thanks to Jane Atkinson, Director, Equestrian Events (Rolex Kentucky); Michael Etherington-Smith, course designer for the Kentucky Rolex Three-Day Event; Willie May, Executive Assistant, Equestrian Events; and Jo Whitehouse, the United States Combined Training Association, for their most generous assistance.

RL 5, 009–012

GOLD MEDAL HORSE
A Bantam Skylark Book / May 1996

ISBN 0-553-48366-8

Published simultaneously in the United States and Canada

PRINTED IN THE UNITED STATES OF AMERICA
OPM   0 9 8 7 6 5 4 3 2 1

*I would like to express my special thanks
to Kimberly Brubaker Bradley
for her help in the writing of this book.*

LISA ATWOOD'S EYES popped wide open. She covered the bottom of the phone with her hand. "Southwood is trying out for the Olympics," she squealed to her two best friends, Stevie Lake and Carole Hanson.

"Really?" Carole and Stevie shrieked at the same time.

"Not the next Olympics, either," Lisa continued breathlessly. "This one! This summer!"

"Really!" Carole and Stevie shrieked again. Stevie jumped to her feet and began pacing.

"Best of all"—Lisa's face lit with excitement—"Drew says Dorothy and Nigel have invited us to come along!"

"We're going," Carole said instantly. Her brown eyes shone. "When do we leave?"

Stevie threw herself back on Lisa's bed, stunned. "The Olympic tryouts?" she repeated. "The Olympics! *This* Olympics?"

Lisa uncovered the phone receiver. "We're pretty excited," she said into it. "Now, tell me all the details." She leaned back into her armchair and tucked her feet beneath her.

"Tell *us* all the details!" Stevie said. She drummed her heels impatiently into the thick pile carpeting. It was a rainy day in early April, and Lisa had chicken pox. Stevie and Carole had come to visit her. Feeling sick and scratchy for a whole week had depressed Lisa's usually bubbly spirits. Now, looking at Lisa's pox-covered but excited face, Stevie thought that the phone call from Drew was exactly what Lisa needed.

"Where are we going?" Carole asked, pulling on Lisa's sleeve to get her attention.

Lisa, murmuring, "Uh-huh, sounds great—sounds *terrific*," pushed Carole's hand away gently and held up one finger.

"We can't wait a minute," Stevie grumbled. "Southwood in this Olympics! Quit chatting and tell us." Patience was not one of Stevie's strong points. Persistence, determination, a love of practical jokes, and an even

2

greater love of horseback riding were Stevie's character-
istics.

Carole rolled her eyes. "If we were at your house, we
could use the speaker phone," she said to Stevie. Stevie's
parents were lawyers, and even their home phones were
loaded with gadgets.

"If we were at my house, Lisa wouldn't be there,"
Stevie said. Lisa was almost recovered, but she wasn't allowed to go outside yet.

"If we were at your house, and Lisa wasn't there, then
we'd already know what was going on. Lisa wouldn't be
able to hog the phone." Carole gave Lisa another impatient grin. Normally Carole was relaxed, but the words
"Southwood" and "Olympics" had her burning to know
more. Carole loved everything about horses, and someday
she wanted to be a professional something-with-horses (a
rider, a trainer, a vet, or a breeder, she wasn't quite sure).
She especially loved Southwood, a beautiful bay
Thoroughbred owned by their friends Dorothy DeSoto
and Nigel Hawthorne. She had ridden Southwood in one
of his very first shows.

"Yeah," Stevie agreed, "but if we were at my house, and
Lisa wasn't there, then I'd have to be talking to Dorky
Drew." She said it quietly so that Drew, who was on the
phone with Lisa, wouldn't overhear. Drew was a dork, but
he was nice, and besides, he worked for Dorothy and

Nigel. Stevie didn't want to insult him—at least not to his face.

Lisa hung up the phone. "Don't call him a dork," she said, turning back to her friends. "He's nice. He's just a little weird and goofy-looking."

"Exactly," Stevie said. "Dorky. Carole, don't you agree?"

Carole smiled. "Yes, but I can't believe you're wasting time talking about it. Lisa! What's going on with Southwood?"

Lisa hugged her knees. "It's the best Saddle Club project ever," she said.

"You've said that before," said Stevie.

"That's because they keep getting better and better. And this time it's definitely true!" The three girls had formed The Saddle Club at the start of their friendship, when they'd realized that the things they cared about most were horses and one another. Saddle Club members had to be horse-crazy, and they had to be willing to help one another. Those were the only rules. The Saddle Club had had a lot of projects since it began—most of them horsey, and most of them successful.

"The best project so far," Lisa repeated. "Even better than our trip to North Carolina."

In November the girls had joined their friend Kate Devine and gone to North Carolina to visit Dorothy and

Nigel. The two adult riders had been their good friends ever since The Saddle Club had helped arrange their wedding. Long ago Dorothy had taken riding lessons at Pine Hollow, the stable where the girls rode now. Dorothy had grown up to be a championship rider, but an accident had prevented her from competing anymore. Nigel, on the other hand, still competed regularly. He was a championship event rider, and right now Southwood was his best horse. Southwood had Olympic potential.

"Tell us," Stevie urged Lisa.

"You did say *this* Olympics, didn't you?" Carole asked at the same time. "Because, remember, Nigel told us Southwood would try out for the *next* Olympics—the one in four years."

Last fall Southwood had belonged to a young woman named Beatrice, who had talent but the wrong attitude about riding. When she hurt herself in a boating accident and then gave up riding, The Saddle Club felt sorry for her, but not for Southwood. Nigel had bought Southwood from Beatrice, and the girls knew that the horse was in the best of hands.

"*This* Olympics," Lisa confirmed. "Okay, here's the story: Nigel has been invited to ride Southwood in the Special Division Horse Trials of the Kentucky Rolex Three-Day Event!"

"That's a mouthful," Stevie remarked. "The Kentucky Rolex Three-Day Event? Haven't I heard of that?"

"I should hope so," Carole said indignantly. "It's only the biggest, most difficult three-day event in North America!"

Three-day eventing was the ultimate test of a horse's skills. Over three days, the same horse had to compete in the three Olympic equestrian disciplines: dressage, cross-country jumping, and stadium jumping. Only the most athletic and well-rounded horses could do eventing.

"Even I've heard of Kentucky Rolex," Lisa said to Stevie. She hadn't been riding for nearly as long as her friends. Lisa got up, walked to her desk, and pulled a horse calendar off the wall. She flipped to the front cover and showed it to Stevie. "That's at Kentucky Rolex," she said.

"Wow." Stevie stared at the color photograph. A man in a red-and-yellow-striped jersey was jumping a chestnut horse out of a lake and over a huge log in a single bound. "That fence looks even bigger than the ones we saw Southwood jump in North Carolina."

"Definitely. This is big time," Carole said. "So . . . Lisa, I'm thrilled Southwood is going to Rolex. But you haven't said how we can help. And what's the Special Division Horse Trials?"

"Drew told me that it's a special division—"

"Well, that makes sense," Stevie muttered, "since it's called 'Special Division'—"

Lisa ignored her and went on, "—for horses who are under consideration—long-listed, Drew called it—for their Olympic teams. Drew said they were going to jump the same superhard fences as the regular advanced division and ride the same hard dressage test, but not do the steeplechase part of cross-country day. They don't want the horses to get worn out this close to the Olympics.

"Drew said there were a lot of horses invited," Lisa continued. "All the top Americans plus Canadians, and a lot of other international riders. Since Nigel's invited, it means that he and Southwood are being considered for the British team."

"That's fantastic!" said Carole. "Nigel must be thrilled! Or . . ." Carole remembered their trip to North Carolina. Nigel had been very concerned that Beatrice was rushing Southwood. Southwood was talented, but he was only seven years old—still very young to be competing internationally. "Is he? Is Nigel thrilled?"

Lisa shook her head. "Drew said Nigel doesn't really want to ride in the special division," she said. "He was planning on riding Southwood in the regular division at Rolex, but he wanted to go slowly and carefully, to make it a learning experience for Southwood. He doesn't want to try for the Olympics!"

7

"But that's crazy!" Stevie declared.

"No, it isn't," Carole said. "I really understand how Nigel feels. If he rushes Southwood, he might scare him, and event horses have to be brave. Nigel could mess Southwood up if he rode him too hard."

"And Nigel would never do that," Lisa concluded. "You're right. But Dorothy and Drew think that Nigel is being overly cautious. They think Southwood is ready. Drew said that Dorothy talked Nigel into riding in the special class at Rolex, but Nigel is insisting that he's going to take it easy. He isn't going to ride Southwood to win. He doesn't want to push him while he's still so young."

The girls thought about this. "But that division will be full of people who want to be in the Olympics," Carole said. "If Nigel takes it easy, he and Southwood won't have a chance."

"Exactly," Lisa said. "So Drew says we shouldn't expect Southwood to actually make the team. But he said that they all thought we'd enjoy the trip to Rolex. Nigel told him he needs at least one of us there to braid Southwood's mane." The girls smiled at one another, appreciating the joke. Nigel always braided his own horse's mane for competition, but he hated doing it. Carole and Stevie had helped him in the fall.

"When is Rolex?" Stevie asked, sitting back down on the bed. She would need another scheme to get her parents to let her go. Fortunately she had several good ideas that she hadn't used yet. Maybe if she—

Lisa grinned. "In two weeks. We'll be gone a whole week."

"But that's spring break!" Stevie clamped her hand over her mouth. What luck! Even though she went to a different school than Carole and Lisa, this year they all had the same spring break.

"Exactly." Lisa smiled. "Dorothy's going to call our parents this evening to ask if we can go, but you know they'll let us. Why wouldn't they?"

Stevie shook her head. "I can't believe that Kentucky Rolex and both our spring breaks are the very same week." She lay back on Lisa's bed. "Coincidences like this are omens. It's foreordained. We're meant to go there. We're meant to help Southwood make the Olympic team."

"I told you," Lisa said.

"Told us what?" Stevie asked.

Carole, grinning, answered for Lisa. "This is the best Saddle Club project ever."

TWO WEEKS LATER, The Saddle Club met at Pine Hollow in the utter blackness of an early-spring morning. It was cool and damp, and even though she was dressed warmly, Carole found herself shivering with excitement. Kentucky Rolex! Southwood, Nigel, the Olympics! Carole thrilled at the thought of all the great horses, great riders, and great riding she would see.

"I wonder where Dorothy is?" Stevie asked impatiently. She checked her watch. They were waiting in the driveway, under the stable's big spotlight, so that they would see Nigel's horse trailer the second it arrived.

"It's early yet," Lisa said soothingly. She brushed a piece of her hair back behind her ear and tried to feel as relaxed as she sounded. "Gosh! When did they say they'd get here?"

"Five-thirty," Stevie said gloomily, "and it's already five-twenty-nine."

"One more minute," Lisa said brightly. Stevie sighed.

Carole jumped as a sudden thought occurred to her. "I don't think I packed my hoof pick!" she said. She dashed into the dark stable. The others could hear her fumbling for the light switch.

Stevie and Lisa laughed. "I think Dorothy and Nigel will remember to bring hoof picks," Lisa said. "Did Carole pack *all* her grooming gear?"

"Probably," Stevie said. "The question is, did she pack underwear?" They laughed again. Carole never forgot anything about horses, but she was famous for being forgetful where she herself was concerned. Once she'd shown up at Pony Club still wearing her pajamas, and she never managed to remember her toothbrush no matter where she went. Both Stevie and Lisa now kept extra toothbrushes at their houses for when Carole spent the night.

Carole came back and stuffed a small metal pick into the top of her duffel bag. Lisa and Stevie peered over Carole's shoulder. Sure enough, the bag was packed with

11

brushes, sponges, lead ropes, and what looked like Carole's good halter. "Underwear?" Stevie inquired.

Carole waved her hand. "In there somewhere. I promise," she added, catching the looks her friends gave her.

"Toothbrush?" Lisa asked.

Carole grinned. "Dorothy said she'd bring an extra one for me. I gave Starlight another hug," she added, referring to her horse. "I hugged Belle and Prancer, too. I hope they don't miss us too much." Belle was Stevie's horse, and Prancer was the lesson horse that Lisa usually rode.

"We've ridden them so much in the past few days, I'm sure they'll be okay," Lisa said.

"They'll be okay," Stevie said. "The question is, will we? A week without horses?"

"Without horses! What about Southwood?" Carole sounded indignant.

Stevie looked mischievous. "I hate to say this, Carole, but I think the days when you—or I or Lisa—rode Southwood are over. He's outgrown us."

"He's older than we are," Carole said. "He's twenty-eight in horse years."

"Is that like dog years?"

"Shorter. Four horse years in a people year."

"Did you girls remember your raincoats?" asked a rich voice behind them.

"Oh, hi, Mrs. Reg!" Pine Hollow Stables was owned

and run by a man named Max Regnery. His mother, Mrs. Regnery, helped him manage the stables. She always looked out for the young riders, and she'd been happy for The Saddle Club when she'd learned of their trip to Kentucky.

"You're up early," Lisa said.

"I didn't want to miss Dorothy. And I hope you did remember raincoats, because the last time I was at Kentucky Rolex, it poured," Mrs. Reg said. "You'll need them."

"It won't rain," Stevie declared. "Rain and mess up our trip? I don't think so!"

"It won't mess up your trip, it'll just mess up your clothes," Mrs. Reg said. "They'll still run the event in the rain. It's in a lovely park, you know—Rolex is held at the Kentucky Horse Park, the only state park dedicated to horses. They built it for the 1978 Eventing World Championship."

"When were you there?" Lisa asked her.

"After 1978, but still before any of you were old enough to sit on a pony," Mrs. Reg said. "In my wild and well-traveled middle age. Let me know when Dorothy arrives, will you? I'm going to make her some coffee." She went into the stable office.

"Five-thirty-four," Stevie said despairingly, looking at her watch. "They'll never get here."

"I wish my spots were gone," Lisa said. Though she was over her chicken pox, her face and arms were still marked with little not-quite-healed red scabs. Her doctor had assured her that they would go away in time. "I feel like I have zits everywhere."

"No one will even notice," Carole assured her. "Where we're going, nobody knows you anyway."

Lisa gave a start. "Oh, I forgot to tell you!" she said. She grimaced. "Drew called again last night. Remember his little brother, the one he was always telling me I was perfect for?"

"Edmund?" asked Stevie. "Wasn't his name Edmund?"

"Edwin. Edwin Gustafs."

"That's right. 'Dready Eddy.'" Stevie recalled the nickname she'd made up when they'd first heard about Drew's younger brother. None of The Saddle Club had ever met him.

"Well," Lisa continued, "it's his spring break, too, up in Maine, so he's coming with us! He flew down to Dorothy and Nigel's last night. Drew is thrilled—he just knows I'll love Eddy."

Stevie made gagging noises.

"He could be nice," Lisa said.

"More likely, he'll be weird. Edwin? Drew's brother? Weird all the way," declared Stevie.

14

"I know." Lisa sighed. "'Dready Eddy' sounds about right, because I'm dreading meeting him. I like Drew fine as a friend, but I really don't want to get fixed up with his little brother."

"We'll take care of you," Carole promised. "We won't leave you alone with him." Lisa looked grateful.

"Five-thirty-eight," muttered Stevie.

A battered green station wagon turned into the driveway. "That can't be Dorothy," Carole said.

Lisa recognized the driver. "It is! But where's Southwood? Where's the horse trailer?"

Dorothy parked, got out of the car, and greeted them with enthusiastic hugs. "Glad to see you!" she said. As the girls trailed Dorothy to the house where she headed to say hello to Mrs. Reg, Dorothy explained that she'd decided to pick them up separately. "We wouldn't all fit in Nigel's truck, and anyway, we wanted Southwood to have as short a ride as possible. Drew and Eddy decided to keep Nigel company, since I'd have the three of you with me for most of the way."

"Great!" Lisa said enthusiastically. The longer she could avoid Eddy, the better. "I mean," she added, seeing the puzzled look that Dorothy gave her, "great that we'll be with you. We'll get to see Nigel tonight."

"And Drew and Eddy," Dorothy said. "Eddy's really

15

looking forward to meeting all of you—and Drew thinks you'll really like him, Lisa. Nigel and I like him a lot—he's so much like Drew!"

"Super," Lisa said in a faint voice. She picked up her duffel bag and opened the back door of Dorothy's car.

"Don't worry," Stevie said into Lisa's ear, "we'll keep you away from him."

Lisa smiled. She knew she could count on her friends.

AFTER A LONG drive, Dorothy and The Saddle Club arrived in Lexington, Kentucky, in the late afternoon. "Not much farther now," Dorothy assured them. Carole leaned her head against the window. They had taken turns sitting in front, and it had been her turn after they'd last stopped for gas. She was tired. She could hardly imagine how tired Dorothy must be—she'd told the girls she'd gotten up at two A.M.

The book Carole was reading slipped from her hand. She reached between her feet to get it and picked up a piece of paper along with the book. When she turned it over, she realized that it wasn't actually a piece of paper.

17

It was a photograph, of a tall, dappled gray horse and Drew.

"Dorothy?" Carole said, holding it out to her.

Dorothy glanced over. "Oh!" she said. "Drew must have left that in here by accident. Put it in the glove box, please, Carole."

Carole quickly showed the photo to her friends and then stowed it away. "Is that one of Nigel's horses?"

Dorothy shook her head a little sadly. "That was Drew's horse, Prospero. Drew had to sell him several years ago, and now he can't find any trace of him. It's as if the horse has disappeared. Drew's very unhappy about it."

"That's sad," Carole said. She wondered why Drew would sell a horse if he didn't want to.

She pressed her face against the cool glass. The clouds that had covered Willow Creek still hung low and thick in the sky. But here in Kentucky the fields and hills seemed even greener than they had in Virginia. The green glowed beneath the leaden sky. Carole shifted slightly. The hills were beautiful.

"I thought Kentucky was the Bluegrass State," said Stevie's voice from the backseat.

"They say it's blue in the very early spring," Dorothy replied. "I don't know. We're never here before Rolex."

"It's green now," Carole said. They'd all enjoyed their trip west. Dorothy had asked them so many questions about their horses and their riding that they'd hardly talked about Southwood at all. Once Carole got talking about Starlight she was hard to stop—and Lisa and Stevie had been just as enthusiastic about Prancer and Belle. They'd chatted for hours. The nice thing, Carole realized, was that Dorothy really wanted to hear about what they had been doing. Even though Dorothy had been a world-class rider, she was still a regular person, and she was a good friend. Carole knew they'd have plenty of time this week to talk about Southwood.

"Hey, look at that," Lisa said. Carole sat up straighter and looked. Along one side of the highway, a perfect white rail fence enclosed acres of lush green pasture. Driving through Kentucky, they'd passed some magnificent Thoroughbred breeding farms, but this looked like the nicest one yet. The car crested a small hill on the highway. Set back behind miles of white fence was a group of stable buildings with beautiful rooflines and tall, elegant spires. It was the biggest, loveliest farm any of them had ever seen.

"What is it?" Carole asked. She'd heard of some of the famous racing stables, where Kentucky Derby winners lived. "Calumet Farm?"

Dorothy smiled. She exited the highway and turned onto a smaller road toward the farm's driveway. "It's the Kentucky Horse Park," she said.

"Wow!" Carole said.

"We'll be staying at a Thoroughbred breeding farm with some friends of ours," Dorothy told them as she turned her car into the long drive. "So you'll see a working Kentucky farm, too."

The horse park seemed like a real farm. The girls could see horses—all kinds of horses, from giant draft horses to tiny foals—in pastures on both sides of the drive. Ahead were some administrative buildings, some farm buildings, and a parking lot. Behind the buildings on the right side was a sea of tents.

As Dorothy turned and drove her car past the buildings, she explained that the tents were part of the setup for the three-day event. Later in the week, there'd be a fair with lots of horsey items for sale, and there'd be a big crowd of spectators once the competition was under way. But there were always tourists at the park. It was open year-round for visitors.

"They have a lot of different horse shows here," Dorothy said. "Kentucky Rolex is the most famous, but there are regular hunter and jumper shows here, too. The Pony Club headquarters are here, and the national Pony Club festival is held here every three years. But besides all that, they've got a lot of permanent attractions. You girls will have time to visit everything."

Dorothy parked near stables surrounded by a chain-link

fence, and they all got out of the car. It felt good to stretch after sitting still so long. "The horses for the advanced and special divisions are housed in here," Dorothy said. "They're valuable animals, so they're well protected. I don't think anyone here would intentionally hurt a horse, but so many spectators come to see Rolex that accidents could happen."

Dorothy sighed. "Unfortunately, access to the stables is tightly controlled. Only owners, riders, and one groom per horse are allowed inside, and that means only Drew, Nigel, and I can go to Southwood's stall. I'll go in now and bring Nigel out to say hi."

"Rats," Carole said, after Dorothy left. "I won't need my hoof pick after all."

"You never know," Lisa said. "I'm sure Southwood won't be in his stall the whole time. Remember how we helped Kate and Nigel at the last event?" She looked around with satisfaction. The area was bustling—horses, riders, grooms—and it smelled like hay and dirt and horse, some of her favorite smells in the world.

Lisa had taken up horseback riding because her mother thought it was something every refined young lady should know. Everyone, including Lisa, had been surprised at how much she had loved it. Lisa's mother would think that these horses and this dirt smelled awful. Lisa was happy to be spending a week surrounded by people who totally understood her love of horses. And she didn't feel as if anyone noticed her spots at all.

"Lisa!" Drew came out of the stable with a big grin on his face. As soon as he saw the rest of The Saddle Club, he greeted them, too, but he seemed happiest to see Lisa. "Oh, gosh," he said with concern, "what happened to your face?"

Lisa frowned. So much for no one noticing! "Chicken pox," she said.

"Oh, that's right, I forgot. I'm so excited that you and Eddy are actually going to meet. He's at the trailer—I'll go get him."

"Wonderful," Lisa said as they watched Drew's lanky frame hurry off.

Dorothy brought Nigel out a moment later, and the girls greeted him with joy. Nigel was every bit as nice as Dorothy, and he always seemed pleased to spend time with The Saddle Club. Like Dorothy, he really cared about them.

Nigel ran his hand through his close-cropped hair and grinned, the smile lighting his intense blue eyes. "Doro tell you about the stabling? Pity you can't go inside." Nigel was British. The Saddle Club loved his crisp accent and the way he called Dorothy 'Doro.' "We even thought about naming one of you as groom," Nigel continued, "but how could we pick between you? Plus, we couldn't

22

do that to Drew. It'd break his heart not to be here with Southwood."

"We understand entirely," Stevie said. "Don't worry."

"Drew knows Southwood best," Carole said. "He'd be able to tell if something was wrong with him long before any of us could. Besides"—she blushed—"I don't think any of us would be quite comfortable taking care of an Olympic horse."

Nigel snorted. Dorothy grinned. "He isn't an Olympic horse," Nigel said.

"Potential Olympic horse," Lisa corrected Carole. Stevie nodded.

Nigel sighed. "I see Doro's recruited you three for her side," he said.

"I think I'll go take another look at Southwood," Dorothy said. She ducked into the stable, leaving the girls alone with Nigel.

Nigel certainly didn't look angry, but he didn't look very happy, either. He seemed to be expecting the girls to argue with him about Southwood's going to the Olympics.

Stevie, in fact, was ready to argue. All through the drive from Virginia, she'd rehearsed in her head reasons why Nigel should ride Southwood for glory. But now, looking at Nigel in front of the Rolex barn, Stevie felt her convincing reasons evaporate. She realized suddenly that

Nigel, a champion rider, knew a lot more about riding than she did. He knew a lot more about Southwood than she did, too.

For a moment none of The Saddle Club spoke. Stevie guessed that her friends were probably thinking the same thoughts she was.

"Dorothy told us about the Special Division Horse Trials," Stevie said at last. "She said you and Southwood are being considered for the British Olympic Equestrian Team." Stevie waited to hear what Nigel would have to say.

Nigel sighed. "You want to know all about it, don't you?" he asked. They nodded. "Well," he said, "I appreciate your not just jumping in and telling me I'm wrong. To Dorothy's credit, she's not doing that, either. She helps me train Southwood, but since I ride him she's letting me have the final say. Ditto Drew. But I know Dorothy thinks I'm being overly cautious." Nigel motioned them to the side of the stabling. They sat down on a small bench made from a log.

"I honestly never thought about riding Southwood in the upcoming Olympics until the day that I was invited to go in the Special Division Horse Trials," he said. "Southwood and I are eligible to ride for Britain. I'm still a citizen, and always will be, and since Southwood is officially owned by our farm, he's got a sort of dual citizenship. Southwood meets all the international and Olympic rules governing horse sports, too—he's old enough, just barely, and he's competed in enough difficult events."

Nigel grinned. "Have you ever heard of the Jamaican bobsled team?" he asked. Stevie nodded, but the others shook their heads. "A bunch of guys from Jamaica entered the Winter Olympics as a bobsled team," Nigel said. "They didn't know what they were doing, and they crashed and finished dead last, but they were amusing. That sort of thing can't happen in the equestrian competitions. The rules make sure that all the horses are capable of international-level competition. Otherwise, they could get hurt."

Nigel quit smiling. He rubbed his chin and looked thoughtful. "I agree with Dorothy that Southwood has Olympic potential," he said. "He's a superstar athlete, the kind of horse that you don't find too often. He's got everything going for him—talent, speed, and temperament.

"Where Dorothy and I disagree is over the word 'potential,'" Nigel continued. "She thinks he could be ready now. I think he's got a long way to go." He tugged the end of Carole's braid. "Max tells me the three of you have potential," he said.

"Yet none of us is ready for the Olympics," Carole said seriously. She felt as if she were answering a question Nigel had asked.

Nigel nodded. "So, you understand. I'm glad. I thought I'd spend the whole week with the three of you trying to change my mind."

The Saddle Club exchanged slightly guilty glances. On the way to Lexington they'd discussed ways to make Nigel change his mind. Dorothy had even said that she wanted their help.

Nigel stretched his arms and continued, in a less serious tone, "I never thought I'd be picked for Britain while I was here in America, anyway," he said. "We're tremendous snobs, you know. We've got the two best events in the world in Britain, and we expect the Americans and everyone else to come to us."

"So why aren't you in England?" Stevie asked.

Nigel grinned. "Dorothy's here," he said. "We've got our farm here, too, and our students. You know I go to England for part of each summer."

"Of course," said Lisa. "That's where we saw you ride Pound Sterling."

"Of course," Nigel said. "Well, what I'd planned on doing was to go back to England in about three years and spend the whole year there, leading up to that Olympics. Now . . . I just don't know. If Southwood were ready, this would be a great year for me to have a chance at the team. A lot of the top British eventers are unavailable just now. Our very best rider is pregnant, and a few others are injured.

"Also, for the first time this year they're taking six people per event team instead of the usual four. The opportunities are greater for me this year, and if Southwood were ready, I'd be thrilled."

They sat in silence for a moment. "Can't you *make* Southwood ready?" Stevie asked. Even before she asked it, she knew the answer. You couldn't make a horse be anything. All training had to be done at the horse's own speed. Stevie understood that best of all The Saddle Club, because she'd once pushed Belle harder than she should have. Fortunately, she'd realized what she was doing before she'd really upset her horse.

"You know I can't," Nigel said gently. "The only way Southwood is going to become the best horse he can be is if I don't push him too hard. He'll have to learn at his own pace."

Nigel gave the bench a thump and stood. "I'm glad we talked about all this right away," he said. "I wanted you to understand why I'm not keen about this particular Olympics. Ordinarily, of course, I'd love to go. It's a dream of a lifetime. But right this minute I've got to run to the stable office and order more shavings for Southwood's stall. And look—here come Drew and Eddy! I'll see you girls soon!"

27

"Duck!" whispered Stevie. She pulled Lisa and Carole around the corner of the fence. They could see Nigel stop and talk to Drew, but they couldn't see Eddy at all. Nigel was blocking him from their view. They could see Nigel point in their direction. "Run!"

They sprinted down the long side of the stable fence and ducked around the corner. "That was close," Carole panted.

"They still might have seen us," Stevie pointed out. "We need to get farther away from them."

"The dreaded Dready Eddy!" Lisa giggled. "It's like a horror movie! What if we go look at some of the horse park buildings? Dorothy said the show passes she gave us would get us into everything."

"Great idea." They crept around the second edge of the stables and sprinted across the road, ducking behind a parked car. They scuttled in and out among the cars until they were well past the stabling area.

"I can see Drew," Stevie said, peering behind them. "He's still by the entrance. But I can't see Eddy. Let's keep moving."

Soon they were well away and could walk comfortably along the road. "Look!" Carole pointed out a small cross-country fence tucked into a hillside. "There are fences everywhere," she said, glancing around. All of the stretches of open ground seemed to contain several cross-country fences. Some were big and some were small. "Look over there—Starlight and I could jump that one."

"Dorothy said they hold a lot of competitions here," Lisa said. "Since the fences are solid, I bet they don't bother to tear them down. It would be a lot of work."

"I bet they recycle them," Stevie said.

"Sure," Carole said. "Dorothy told me that every year they change part of the Rolex course, but they never change it all at once. It would be too much work."

"This place is beautiful," Lisa said. "If we can just keep away from Dready Eddy, I'm sure we'll have a great time. But I do feel a little bad about what Nigel said. I mean, suddenly I don't feel like we're going to be able to change his mind. I'd been thinking we could make him a Saddle Club project."

"I'm not sure we should try to change his mind," Carole said. "Everything he said just now made sense. And he does know a lot about horses."

"Yes, but so does Dorothy," Stevie argued. "She thinks Southwood can do it, and remember, even if she doesn't ride, she's just as good a horseperson as Nigel. I understand Nigel's point of view now, but I still think we should try to change it. Maybe," she added as she remembered how convincing Nigel had been. "Anyway, we've got the whole week."

"That's right," said Lisa. "We can think about it some more and decide what's best to do."

"A plan," Stevie said, her eyes mischievous. "Nigel has a plan for Southwood. We'll make a plan to change his plan."

"*If* we decide that Dorothy's right," Carole said. "Since we can see both sides of the argument, it's hard to know what to do." Stevie and Lisa agreed.

4

ON TUESDAY MORNING Stevie woke, stretched, and then, looking around her, couldn't help grinning. She was lying between crisp white sheets, under a white down comforter, surrounded by blue-and-white-striped walls. Next to her, Carole slept in a similar twin bed, and Lisa slept in nearly equal comfort on a folding cot. White lace curtains billowed in the breeze from the open window. By sitting up, Stevie could get a glimpse through the window of mares grazing peacefully with foals at their sides.

"Blue Hill," Stevie said softly to herself. They were in the second bedroom of the guesthouse at Blue Hill, the

31

most elegant farm The Saddle Club had ever seen. When Dorothy told them that she'd arranged for them all to stay at a friend's house for the week, Stevie had imagined sleeping bags in the hayloft of someone else's stable. She'd never dreamed of a Thoroughbred breeding farm and a mansion complete with a separate house just for guests. Dorothy and Nigel were staying in the guesthouse's other bedroom. The house had two bathrooms and a cozy combination kitchen and living room, with leather chairs and a tiny fireplace. But they weren't expected to cook—Mr. and Mrs. Drake Harrington III, who owned Blue Hill, told them that they were expected for dinner every night when they weren't otherwise engaged.

"Otherwise engaged" had an elegant sound to it, and so did "expected for dinner," but right now what Stevie wanted was breakfast. She woke up Carole and Lisa, and in fifteen minutes they were walking around the edge of the Harringtons' pool, toward the kitchen of the main house.

"Do we knock or walk right in?" Carole asked. She felt a little in awe. At dinner the night before, Mr. and Mrs. Harrington (whom Dorothy and Nigel called "Stelle" and "Harry") had been friendly and kind, but the meal had been served by an honest-to-gosh butler wearing honest-to-gosh livery, and a few of the things Carole had eaten she'd never even heard of before.

32

"Dunno," Stevie said. "I hope they don't serve capers for breakfast. What were those things, anyway? Ducks?"

"I think the chicken stuff was called 'capons,'" Lisa said. "I think the capers were the little round green things."

"Whatever." Stevie sighed. "Dinner was fun, with all the china and the chandelier, and I did like the chicken, but right now I'd prefer a nice, hot cherry Pop-Tart."

"Dinner was nice," Lisa said with a giggle, "but the best part of Blue Hill so far is that Drew and Eddy are staying in the horse trailer at the park. I can't believe we've managed to avoid them this long!"

"Beware the Dready Eddy," Stevie intoned.

"Did you see Nigel's big trailer?" Carole asked. "It's got a little apartment in the front, like a camper. Nigel says he and Dorothy stay in it a lot."

"I saw it," Lisa said. "It's neat. But I'm glad we're here and the boys aren't."

They knocked, and the cook directed them into the same dining room where they'd eaten the night before. It looked only slightly less elegant in the daytime. Seated at the table were two small children wearing private-school uniforms and shoveling cereal into their mouths. The cook introduced them as little Drake and Tory, the Harrington children.

"Hi," Tory said around a mouthful of cereal. She had

33

brown pigtails tied with ribbons, and she looked about six years old. "Do you ride?" she asked.

"Yes," said Lisa, smiling.

Tory looked at her appraisingly. "Do you have your own horse?"

"No." She pointed at Stevie and Carole. "They do."

"Do you want your own horse?"

"Of course," Lisa said.

Tory smiled so suddenly that Lisa felt she'd passed some sort of test. "Okay," the little girl said, and went back to eating cereal. The butler—in regular clothes this time, navy slacks and a white shirt—came in with a tray of orange juice for The Saddle Club and a basket of muffins, which he placed on the table. He offered them their choice of eggs, sausages, or cereal. Stevie, eyeing the muffins, decided she didn't want Pop-Tarts after all. She asked for one egg and two sausages.

"We couldn't stay up for dinner last night because you were late and we had school and because Dad said it had to be just grown-ups, but we wanted to, and we're staying up tonight no matter what," Drake said earnestly, all in a rush. He had short brown hair and dark brown eyes, and he looked about a year older than his sister. "We'll show you our ponies."

"We'd love to see them," Lisa said. "This is the prettiest farm I've ever been to."

34

"We'd love to see some of the foals, too," Carole said. "We really like Thoroughbreds—the horse Lisa rides is a Thoroughbred."

A tall, muscular woman wearing jeans and a cotton sweater walked quickly into the room. "Good morning," she said briskly. "Sleep well?"

"Good morning, Mrs. Harrington," The Saddle Club chorused. Drake and Tory waggled their fingers at their mother.

"I slept well," Tory announced.

"I know that," Mrs. Harrington said. "You've already told me so twice this morning. I was speaking to our guests. Carole, I heard what you just said, and I'll make sure you get a grand tour sometime soon." She smiled at The Saddle Club. "The little foals are delightful, but we'll want to show you our riding horses, too. Now, Tory, Drake, hurry up! It's almost time for the school bus!"

The little kids slurped the last of their milk, kissed their mother, and waved to The Saddle Club before they shot out the door. "Tory—don't forget your lunch!" Mrs. Harrington called after them. She smiled and said, "Thanks," as the butler brought her a cup of coffee.

"I'll take you around Blue Hill soon," she repeated. "This morning, though, I need to leave for the horse park right away, and I thought you'd probably want to come with me. Dorothy and Nigel went over a few hours ago, and I'm sure you're eager to meet up with them."

"And Southwood," Carole agreed. "We hardly saw him at all yesterday." It was the only downside to their game of Hide from Eddy.

On the way to the horse park, Mrs. Harrington explained that she volunteered during Kentucky Rolex. "I serve as an outrider on cross-country day," she said. "My mare and I keep a certain section of the course clear and keep the spectators in line. Also, I can ride for help if anyone, competitor or spectator, needs it." She dropped them off near the stabling area, and Lisa asked someone who was going into the stables to tell Dorothy or Nigel that they were there. Soon Drew came out to meet them. He had four bottles of horse liniment in his hands, and as he came out the door he tripped. A bottle of liniment sloshed down his pant leg.

"Oh, gosh!" he said, ignoring the stinking liniment. "I can't believe it. You just missed Eddy by five minutes! He and Dorothy drove into Lexington to buy a leather lead shank—we forgot to bring one." Drew looked disappointed. Lisa almost felt sorry for him because he so much wanted them to like his brother, but then she imagined a younger version of Drew, with the same goofy wide mouth and uneven eyebrows. *Ugh!* Lisa shook her head.

"I can't believe we keep missing him," she said sincerely, because it was true. Lisa couldn't believe their good luck.

"Where's Nigel?" Carole asked.

"He took Southwood out for a long hack," Drew said. "I just finished cleaning his stall. I need to put these bottles away, and then do you guys want to do something? We could take a trail ride—they have those on the other side of the park."

Lisa thought about it. A trail ride would be on a horse, and it would be an excuse to stay away from Eddy. Both of those things sounded great. She looked at her friends, who nodded. "Let's go!"

It was a long walk to the trail ride, and when they got there, the girls were disappointed. This was nothing like the trail rides they were used to, at home in Pine Hollow or anywhere else. This was a guided horseback ride along a smooth, flat trail—more like a road, really, Carole thought—and the horses followed one another nose-to-tail, at a walk, without needing any cues from their riders. Two other tourists were waiting for rides—an overweight man who could hardly climb into the saddle and a woman wearing shorts and sandals.

"It's like a kiddie ride for grown-ups," Carole whispered. The guide, a lithe young woman, let them pick any horses they liked from the dozen or so tethered at the start. Carole chose a bay, because that was Starlight's color.

"It's still a horse," Lisa whispered back, but she felt sad. These horses probably never got a chance to do fun things, like gallop through woods. They had to carry people who wore sandals and knew nothing about riding. Lisa chose the saddest-looking horse in hopes that she could do something to cheer it up.

Drew chose a gray horse. "Like Prospero," Carole said, remembering.

Drew stared at her. "How did you know that?" he asked. Carole explained about the photo she'd seen. Drew nodded sadly. "I miss him so much," he said. "I just wish I knew that he was doing okay."

Carole nodded sympathetically. She wanted to know more about Prospero, but the ride was beginning.

When they started off, The Saddle Club saw to their surprise that Drew did not ride well at all. Even at a sedate walk, he sat awkwardly and held the reins as if he was uncomfortable. His legs were jammed awkwardly against his horse's side.

Stevie tried not to stare at Drew. Because he worked as a groom and knew so much about horses, she'd always assumed that he knew a lot about riding. Watching him sway crookedly with his neck and feet too far forward, she knew she'd assumed wrong.

"I love horses," Drew said, catching her eye, "but I can't ride at all."

"You look okay," Stevie said lamely. She didn't think she should say she agreed. Drew looked worse than all but the newest beginners at Pine Hollow.

"No, I don't. I'm really awful." The truth didn't seem to bother Drew. "I love horses, but I admitted to myself a long time ago that I don't have any talent in the saddle. I tried hard, but I really can't ride."

"But you know so much about horses," Carole protested. Like Stevie, she found Drew's ineptitude hard to believe.

"I know about them from the ground, I love them, and I take good care of them," Drew said. "I've got a good eye for horses—I can recognize good ones. Someday I'd like to combine all that and be a bloodstock agent, a person who buys and sells horses for a living. But I can't ride."

Drew sat back. His legs inched even farther forward, and his neck was still crooked. Lisa was momentarily glad that the trail horses were so quiet. She'd hate to see Drew get hurt.

"Someday I'll be an agent," Drew repeated dreamily, leaning back even farther. "For now, all I'd like is to see Southwood do his best this weekend. I'd like to see him be *allowed* to do his best."

Drew straightened up. Lisa gave a sigh of relief; she'd been sure he was going to fall right off. "I don't mean to be critical of Nigel," Drew continued. "He takes a conservative approach to horse training, and I think that's good most of the time. But I think Southwood is a truly great horse—and I'm not just saying that because I love him. Horses like Southwood are so rare, and so talented. I really want Southwood to get his chance at a gold medal." Drew shrugged. "In four years, anything could happen. Southwood could get sick, or he could get hurt. This might be his best shot, and I think he should take it."

The tour guide, riding in front of The Saddle Club and Drew, suggested a trot. She told them they could hang on to the horn of their saddles if they felt insecure. All the horses on the ride were outfitted in Western tack.

"As if I would do that!" Stevie said indignantly. The Saddle Club knew from riding at their friend Kate's ranch out West that the horn on a Western saddle was not meant to be a handle. It was used for roping cattle. Besides, no good rider kept his balance by hanging on to part of his tack.

The guide smiled sympathetically. "I don't mean you," she said. "I can see you three know what you're doing. I mean the others." She showed the fat man and the sandaled woman how to hold on.

They set off at a sluggish trot, the horses all imitating the leader's horse. Right away the sandaled woman started shrieking, "I'm bouncing! I'm bouncing!" She *was* bouncing, too. Her backside walloped against the saddle with every stride. Lisa, trotting smoothly, winced on behalf of the woman's horse. The tour guide must have felt sorry for the horse, too, because she quickly brought them all back to a walk. The Saddle Club resumed their conversation with Drew.

"I understand what you're saying," Stevie told him. "But I also know that trying to make a horse learn too fast can really slow its training down or even ruin the horse in the long run, because it could get scared and nervous."

"I've always thought that Dorothy and Nigel were two of the best trainers ever," Carole added.

"Oh, I agree," Drew said. "They are great, but even they don't agree about Southwood. It's hard to know what's best in this case. I think Nigel's concern for Southwood is wonderful, but I also think that Southwood really wants to win." Drew smiled wistfully. "Southwood reminds me of Prospero in that way," he said.

"Tell us about him," Lisa said. They all wanted to hear the story.

"He had a heart of gold," Drew said. "Talking about him brings back so many memories. He was the only horse I've ever owned."

"Why did you have a horse if you didn't ride?" asked Stevie.

"I did ride, I just gave it up," Drew explained. "I took lessons for a long time. Prospero loved to jump, but he was also gentle and obedient. I competed him in preliminary-level events—and given how awfully I ride, that should tell you something about what kind of horse he was. He really took care of me, and he never, ever gave up. He had a champion heart." Drew laughed suddenly. "I taught him to shake hands, too, for a carrot—just like a circus horse! I'd whistle and he'd hold his hoof up, then I'd give him a carrot."

Lisa remembered the difficult event in England that Nigel had told them was "preliminary" level. Looking at the way Drew rode now, she could hardly imagine him galloping over solid fences on any kind of horse. "Prospero really must have been super," she said. "Why did you sell him?"

Drew smiled another sad smile. "He was too good a horse for a rider like me," he said. "He was capable of so much more than I was ever going to be capable of. I loved him, but I knew I was holding him back, so I sold him to a professional rider who could take him to higher levels of competition."

"Then what happened?" Stevie said. "Where is he now?"

Drew shook his head. "That's the worst thing," he said. "I don't know where he is. I tried to keep in touch with him—I wanted to know everything about him—but first he injured a tendon in his leg while galloping in his pasture, and he couldn't be ridden for a year. Then he was sold to a rider in California. I think they must have changed his name, because I never heard a word about him again. It was years ago that I rode him. He could be dead."

Drew looked anguished. "I don't want Nigel to push Southwood," he said, "but I want him to have a chance. What if something happens to him, like it did to Prospero? Prospero should have had a chance."

Lisa looked at her friends. They all felt enormously sad for Drew, who obviously loved Prospero very much. *He loved Prospero enough to sell him to a better rider*, Lisa thought, realizing how much courage that had taken. She remembered when her old beloved lesson horse, Pepper, had grown old and sick. She had made the decision to end Pepper's suffering, and it was one of the hardest and best decisions she'd ever made. Drew's selling Prospero sounded like the same kind of choice.

"I'm so sorry," Carole said softly. "Maybe Prospero's doing really well in California. Maybe he's a champion event horse."

Drew shook his head. "I subscribe to a magazine that

43

covers all the show results. They publish photographs of the winners. I'd recognize him if I ever saw him. Whatever he's doing, he isn't winning." He tightened his reins involuntarily, and his horse tossed its head. "I don't want that to happen to Southwood!"

They had ridden in a loop along the far fence of the horse park and were nearly back to the start of the ride. The Saddle Club was silent, thinking. Finally Stevie spoke.

"None of us knows more than Dorothy or Nigel," she said. "But, Drew, what you say makes at least as much sense as what Nigel said to us last night. We're willing to help you convince Nigel. We'd like to see Southwood do well."

The others nodded. "It's a Saddle Club project," Lisa said.

Drew looked grateful. "Thanks."

5

WEDNESDAY MORNING THE Saddle Club woke up early enough to head to the horse park with Dorothy and Nigel. Nigel had to go to a competitors' meeting, but he invited them all to go on the official course walk with him afterward. Walking the cross-country course was the only way the riders could plan their strategy: The horses weren't allowed to see any of the fences until they were asked to jump them. The Saddle Club had walked a course with Nigel in North Carolina, and they enjoyed seeing all the enormous fences up close.

Dorothy parked her station wagon near the stables, and Nigel hurried off to his meeting. The girls walked with

Dorothy to the stables and were admiring a handsome blood bay horse near the entrance when Drew rushed out to meet them. "Hey!" he said. "You still haven't met Eddy! I know where he is—don't move, I'll go get him!"

Stevie clapped her hand over her mouth and shrieked. "Ohmigosh!" she said. "I left my purse in the station wagon! We've got to run—someone could steal it!" She grabbed Lisa's hand and the three of them fled.

"Stevie," Carole said, gasping, "you don't have a purse."

Stevie grinned. "Quick thinking, wasn't it?"

"Definitely," Lisa replied. They ran past the parking lot and leaned against a tree until they'd caught their breaths. "Now," Lisa said, "what should we do until the course walk?"

On the day before, they'd located the dressage and show-jumping rings, visited the Pony Club's office, and watched a film about horses in the main horse-park building. Lisa pulled a battered park map out of her pocket. "Let's visit the Breeds Barn," she suggested.

As its name indicated, the Breeds Barn was filled with horses of all sorts of breeds, both familiar and rare, from all over the world. The girls walked past stalls containing a Thoroughbred, an Arabian, a Morgan, a quarter horse, a Welsh pony, an Appaloosa, and a Saddlebred. All of those were types of horses they had at Pine Hollow. They

46

paused to admire the different kinds of giant draft horses, the Austrian Lipizzaner, and the Peruvian Paso Fino. Finally they stopped in amazement in front of a stall containing the hairiest pony they'd ever seen. Its mane and forelock cascaded down its neck, and its thick black coat rippled in heavy waves.

"What is it?" Stevie asked. She gave the pony a pat, and it snuffled her hand.

Carole read the card. "'Bashkir Curly.'

"'Bashkiria was a remote area in the former Soviet Union,'" Carole continued to read. "And I guess the curly part is self-explanatory," she said with a giggle.

"I'd say so," Lisa agreed.

Before they knew it, it was time for the course walk. Consulting Lisa's map, they joined Dorothy and Nigel at the second fence to avoid going back near the stables. Fortunately, Lisa thought with relief, Drew was too busy to go on the walk, and Eddy didn't seem to be interested because he hadn't come along.

The Saddle Club had seen difficult cross-country fences before, but these were the hardest yet. While Nigel walked carefully around each obstacle, planning exactly where and how he and Southwood should jump it, the girls climbed on top of each one and marveled that any horse *would* jump it. The fifth fence, called the Footbridge, was built over a ditch and was nearly six feet wide.

47

Stevie stood in the ditch. The rails of the fence were higher than her head. "Awesome," she declared.

Dorothy leaned over a rail and looked down at Stevie. "The horses jump both sides together," she reminded her. "On the outside, the fence is only about four feet tall."

"Oh, only four feet," Lisa muttered with a touch of sarcasm. "That's not much." Four feet! When would she ever jump four feet high—let alone six feet wide!

"What's the purpose of the ditch, then?" Carole asked. Her eyes were gleaming; she loved learning everything about riding. She'd always thought of becoming a show jumper, but eventing thrilled her, too. Maybe she'd do both.

Dorothy laughed. "To scare the rider. The horses won't look at it, probably, unless the rider seems nervous."

"Are you nervous, Nigel?" Lisa asked.

"Right now, no." Nigel grinned. "At three in the morning on the day I have to jump these things, I'll be very nervous. And when it comes time to actually ride, I won't be nervous at all." Dorothy rolled her eyes disbelievingly. "Well," Nigel amended, "maybe a little nervous."

Farther into the course they came to a fence shaped like a giant V laid parallel to the ground. A big tree grew in the middle of the V.

"Dorothy," Carole asked while Nigel walked away from

the fence to study the approach, "you taught us about the flags on the jump—you said the riders had to keep the red flag on their right and the white one on their left. That way they'd always know from which direction to jump the fence."

Dorothy nodded. "That's right."

Lisa saw the problem right away. "On this fence there are two white flags—on the outsides of the V—and only one red flag—on the point in the middle. How do you jump it?"

Dorothy explained. "This is an option fence. You have to jump between all the flags, but in this case you have a choice of two ways. You can go over both arms near the very corner of the V, right against the red flag, in a single jump, or you can jump both arms of the V as separate jumps."

"But there's a tree growing in the middle," Stevie protested. "You'd have to go around it."

"That's right," Dorothy said. "Lots of horses don't like jumping corners, and if you aim too close to the corner of the V you risk having your horse duck around the fence. That costs a lot of penalty points. On the other hand, if you jump the arms separately and go around the tree, it will take much longer. This course has to be ridden at a gallop, and if you go over the time limit you get penalized for that, too."

Nigel came up and was looking at the backside of the V. "Option fences make difficult courses like this suitable for a variety of horses," he said. "The short, direct routes are harder, but the easier routes take longer. If your horse isn't ready for the harder routes, you can still get through the course safely, but you won't be fast enough to win."

"They do that at the Olympics, too," Dorothy said. "They build all the really hard courses with some easier options. They always want the horses to be safe."

"Oh." Carole looked at the fence thoughtfully. "How will you jump this one, Nigel?" Nigel flushed and exchanged glances with Dorothy. Carole realized, to her dismay, that her question made him uncomfortable.

"Southwood could do the fast route, couldn't he?" Stevie asked. Like Carole, she was aware of the faint tension between Dorothy and Nigel. On the other hand, it was a Saddle Club project to get Southwood to the Olympics. "I bet he could, a great horse like him."

"Probably." Nigel gave a small laugh. "Corners are one of the worst types of obstacles," he said. "You have to ride them accurately and absolutely know that your horse will listen to you. I'll—mmm—well, I'll probably go the long route here."

"But it's so long," Carole said before she could stop herself. Nigel looked unhappy, and Carole wished she'd kept quiet.

50

"All the riders memorize all the options on the fences," Dorothy said quietly. "That way they can change their plan in the middle of the course if they have to, if their horse is going worse than they expected—or better." She smiled at Nigel and slipped her arm through his. Nigel looked at her affectionately, and The Saddle Club felt relieved. Dorothy and Nigel felt differently about what Southwood could do, but they weren't quarreling.

At the end of the course walk, Nigel invited them to lunch. "We'll go back to the stables and pick up Drew and Eddy," he said.

"Thanks, but—" Lisa looked at her friends.

"—but we're dying to go on another trail ride," Carole said firmly. "We had such a wonderful time yesterday. And we ate such big breakfasts that we really aren't hungry. Do you mind?"

"Can't keep you off horses, can we?" Nigel said. "Okay, have fun—but don't ask those rental horses to jump any of the fences!"

"I can't believe you said we weren't hungry," Stevie told Carole as they walked across the park. "My stomach's about to eat my liver for lunch."

"What I can't believe is that you said we wanted another trail ride," Lisa said. "Yesterday's was so lame! But thanks, Carole. I don't think I could have thought of an excuse fast enough."

"So far we're definitely winning the game of Dready Eddy," Stevie said. "And look! A hot dog cart!"

After two chili cheese dogs apiece they felt fortified and ready for the trail ride. "Oh, fiery steeds," murmured Stevie as they approached.

This time there weren't any other tourists waiting to ride, and the guide recognized them from the day before. She seemed glad to see them. "Hurry!" she said. "Get on and let's leave, before some more tourists show up and we have to take them."

The girls laughed. "Do you get lots of women in sandals?" Lisa asked.

The guide rolled her eyes. "You wouldn't believe," she said. "But I can tell you all know how to ride."

They started out. Lisa rode her sad horse from the day before, and Carole rode the same bay. Stevie picked a pinto that reminded her a little of Stewball, the horse she rode at her friend Kate's ranch. "Only Stewball has an engine," she said, complaining about the pinto's poky stride. "This horse feels like a motor scooter."

"'A horse is a horse, of course, of course,'" sang Lisa.

"Not when it's a moped," Stevie replied darkly.

Carole used her legs to urge her horse on. "I feel like mine's a bicycle," she said. "I'm doing all the work."

They followed the level path around the side of the

park. Once they'd given the horses a chance to warm up, the guide said they could trot—and when the three girls all rose smoothly to a trot, the three horses perked up their ears and moved more willingly. "Poor ponies," Lisa said soothingly, patting her gray horse. "They're so used to people bouncing on their backs. No wonder they don't want to move."

They turned the corner so that they were now following the fence line along the front of the park. Trucks whooshed down the highway just across the fence, but the trail horses seemed oblivious to them.

Stevie turned in her saddle to speak to Lisa. "This really is bor—Arrhh!" She shrieked as her horse gave a sideways leap and whirled, then stood with muscles trembling, ears pointing toward the fence. "What was that for?"

The other horses jumped, too. For a moment Carole felt her balance slipping. She grabbed her horse's mane and stayed on. *That's what I get for not paying attention*, she scolded herself. She knew a rider could fall off any horse, anytime.

"Oh, no!" Lisa's voice rose high in panic. Suddenly the riders could see what had spooked their horses—a lone horse, a skinny, haggard-looking, almost-white horse, plunging toward them across four lanes of traffic!

A huge semitruck blared its horn. The horse leaped onto the grass median, ran in place for a stride, then dashed onto the other half of the highway. A passenger car slammed on its brakes, swerving around the horse. The horse raised its head and squealed desperately.

"He'll be killed!" Carole screamed.

THE GRAY-WHITE HORSE managed to dart onto the shoulder of the highway. He paused, muscles trembling, then lifted his head and whinnied a high, loud squeal. He took a few determined cantering strides down the tall grassy bank, measured the white fence of the horse park with his eyes, and gathered himself to jump it.

The board fence was not very big—maybe four feet high but skinny and straightforward, not like the wide cross-country fences. The horse was tall, and from the expression on his face and the way he gathered himself together, the girls knew he was putting everything he had into jumping the fence. Carole swallowed hard.

The horse thrust himself into the air. Despite his efforts, he didn't jump high enough to clear the top board. His knees crashed against it. The board broke, and the horse stumbled into the field, right in front of their startled trail horses. He picked himself up and began to run away from them, straight for the stables!

"Stop him!" the trail guide yelled. They all knew how dangerous it would be for a loose horse to gallop into the crowd around the barn. Ahead of the galloping horse were people, cars, champion horses—and the panicked horse could trample them all. He could be hurt, too.

Wheeling their pluggy trail horses, they took off after the renegade. Lisa saw the way the fleeing horse stretched himself into a full gallop, and her heart sank. He reminded her of Prancer—of a Thoroughbred, a horse bred for racing. If that was true, they'd never catch him, not on these old, plain trail horses.

She leaned forward and urged her horse on with her heels. Beside her, Carole crouched low over the black mane of her bay. Stevie's pinto was snorting. Lisa's horse picked up speed and galloped with real enthusiasm. She felt his hooves thud against the ground. The ground became a blur.

And the renegade was slow. Despite his elegant gait and his long, ground-swallowing stride, the girls began to close the gap between their horses and him.

"Hi-yi-yi!" Stevie shouted encouragement to her mount. She wished she had a rope so that she could lasso the white horse the way she'd learned to on Kate's ranch. Within a few more strides they'd reached the horse and were galloping alongside him, but Stevie didn't see how they were ever going to stop him.

Carole wasn't sure, either. She tried the only thing she could think of: She rode close to the gray-white horse, grabbed his long mane with one hand, and said, "Whoa," in a loud, firm voice. To her surprise, it worked. The horse stopped as suddenly as he'd started.

All four of them, including the guide, brought the trail horses to a halt. "I'll be," the guide said to Carole. "I didn't think that would work. For a runaway, he's sure obedient!"

Carole nodded. They surrounded the horse. He stood politely, but he continued to look in the direction of the stables, and he raised his head and trumpeted again. He sounded so sad and so full of longing that she felt a great lump of sorrow rise in her throat. The poor horse!

Carole slipped off her mount and handed her reins to the guide. Talking quietly to the gray-white horse, she checked him over from head to toe. The more she looked, the more depressed she felt. One of the horse's knees had been scratched by the fence board, but other than that he

57

didn't seem to have been hurt during his wild trip across the highway.

However, it was obvious that he'd been hurt many times in the past. "Look at his legs," Carole whispered. They bore the marks of several old injuries: His back tendons, which should have been tight and smooth, were marred by several ugly bumps. "He's got scars all over him. No wonder he couldn't jump high or run fast."

"Look at his shoulders," Lisa said. "He looks just like Prancer. I'm sure he's a Thoroughbred."

"Look at his face," Stevie said. "He's quality. I bet he used to be a really good horse. He looks old, though—and he's so skinny!"

"He must be old," the guide interjected. "See how his face bones stand out and his back sways?"

"He's sweet," Carole added, rubbing the horse's nose. "He stopped when we asked him to, even though he wanted to run." She ran her hand down the horse's neck. There were scars there, too, and more on his flanks that looked as if they'd been caused by a sharp whip or spurs. "Poor baby. What should we do with him?"

"He came from across the highway," Stevie said. "I think we should take him back there and try to find his owner."

"His owner!" Carole sounded indignant. "Look at him! He's *too* skinny, too, and he sure doesn't look like anyone's been taking good care of him. In fact"—Carole looked the horse up and down—"I'd say that he's been abused. I don't think we should take him back to his owner! I think we should take care of him ourselves!"

Stevie looked at Carole thoughtfully. "Lisa?" she asked. "What do you think we should do?"

Lisa looked at the horse sadly. His sorry condition reminded her a little of Sal, an abused horse she had once met. Sal had been rescued, but he had died because of the horrible treatment he'd received and because he hadn't gotten help until it was too late. "I would never want to put him back in a bad situation," she said slowly, "and I'm sure not keen about going across that highway. But, Carole, he doesn't look that bad. None of his scars are fresh. I don't think we can judge this horse's owner without meeting him or her."

Lisa made up her mind. "Here's what I think we should do: take the horse back, and talk to its owner. If we think the horse isn't getting good care, we can tell Dorothy and Nigel, and they'll help us get help for it."

Even the guide agreed with Lisa's plan. Carole took off her belt and looped it around the white horse's neck. The others took off their belts, too, and Carole buckled them together to make a sort of lead rope. Carole remounted, and they led the horse back to the break in the rail fence. The white horse looked anxiously over his shoulder a few times, but he followed without giving them trouble. "Such a good boy," Carole murmured to him.

They stood before the gap in the fence. With the top rail broken, the fence was about two and a half feet high.

"Do the horses know how to jump?" Carole asked the guide.

Stevie looked determined. "We'll find out."

The guide laughed. "I don't think so," she said. "These horses can't leave the park. Let me hold them, and you guys can walk our buddy across the road. I'll wait for you here."

Carole climbed over the broken portion of the fence, still holding the gray-white horse's lead, and clucked to him encouragingly. The horse looked over his shoulder and whinnied sadly once again, then tucked himself together and jumped the fence from a halt. This time he cleared it. The girls waited for a break in the traffic, then quickly led him across the road.

On the far shoulder they stopped in surprise. They'd never noticed it, but the other side of the highway was dotted with small pastures, too, just like the horse park. Only here the fences were made of sturdy brown rails, and the buildings behind them looked plain and utilitarian. A number of horses grazed in the pastures, and they raised their heads curiously to look at the gray-white horse. Before Stevie and Carole could do more than look at the horses in return, a red Jeep tore down the driveway, screeching to a halt right in front of them.

"You got him!" A man in a brown leather jacket exclaimed in relief as he parked the Jeep and got out. "Is he okay?" He took the lead from Carole and ran his hands quickly over the gray-white horse's legs. Then he looked at the three girls. "Are *you* okay? What happened?"

They described the horse's jump, chase, and capture. "I'm grateful to you," the man said. "You did exactly the right thing. I'm Dr. Lawrence. I'm a vet, and this is the Kentucky Equine Hospital. Ghost here is one of our patients."

The girls shook his hand and introduced themselves. "'Ghost' is a good name for him," Stevie said. "He looks like a ghost—tall and white and thin."

Dr. Lawrence looked thoughtful. "Yes, that's why I named him that," he said. "I have no idea what his real name is. He's a registered Thoroughbred, but he's so old that the numbers on his lip tattoo have faded and you can't read them. I don't know where he came from originally. He was a rescue from the SPCA."

Carole's eyes sparked angrily. "I knew he'd been treated badly!"

Dr. Lawrence nodded. "Unfortunately, yes. The man from whom we got him hadn't owned him long, however. Most of Ghost's injuries look old, and many of them aren't actually the result of poor care. He just got hurt, probably—like a football player blowing out his knee."

Dr. Lawrence began leading Ghost back to the hospital building, and the girls followed. "This horse has been pacing up and down the pasture, looking at the horse park, ever since he got here," he told them. "Today he finally jumped his fence. I keep thinking maybe he's an old event horse trying to get back to competition. Maybe he remembers Rolex."

Carole liked the idea but doubted it was true. "That sounds too much like a fairy tale," she said. "But he did try awfully hard to jump into the park—you could tell he tried as hard as he could."

"He's got a lot of spirit, but he's still obedient," Stevie added. "He stopped as soon as we asked him to. He's a good horse."

Dr. Lawrence led the horse through a large door into a stable with large stalls. "We'll keep him inside and keep an eye on him," he said. He gave the horse a few flakes of hay, and soon the horse was munching happily. "He's a mystery, that's for sure," Dr. Lawrence said. "He's not a young horse—see how his gray coat has faded to almost pure white?—and with those legs he'll always be somewhat lame. I'm sure he's had a hard life, but I agree with you. I think he's a good horse."

Carole ran her hand through the horse's long mane.

"What happens to him now?" she asked. "Can he stay here?"

Dr. Lawrence sighed. "Not permanently, but certainly for a while longer," he said. "I'd like to find a good retirement home for him, but it won't be easy. Someone will have to take this old boy out of the goodness of his or her heart." Dr. Lawrence shook his head sadly.

"Our friends Dorothy and Nigel know a lot of riders," Stevie suggested. "Maybe they'd know someone who could take him. We'll ask." She patted Ghost's neck. "He sure is a nice horse."

"If you have any ideas for a home, call me," Dr. Lawrence said gratefully. "I really appreciate your rescuing and returning him. Thank you."

"Well," Carole said to Lisa as they walked back, "you were right—he's in good hands now."

"Now," Stevie admitted, "but not forever. Ghost needs a permanent home."

Carole nodded, frowning. They'd have to think of something.

"BUT I THOUGHT it was called a three-day event," Stevie protested. "Why is Nigel's dressage test on Thursday, when cross-country doesn't start until Saturday and the show jumping is on Sunday?"

"That makes it a four-day event," Lisa said. They were on their way to Rolex with Dorothy. Nigel had already gone ahead to get ready for the first phase of the competition.

"There are too many competitors," Dorothy said. "To make the competition fair, all of the horses have to be judged by the same dressage judges, and they can't fit them all into a single day, so they spread the tests over two days. It doesn't matter—Southwood still has to be obedient and supple today and bold over cross-country on Saturday."

"And show jumping on Sunday," Carole supplied.

"Yes." Dorothy nodded. "More than anything else, the show jumping proves that the horse hasn't been completely worn out from cross-country day."

"Will Nigel do well in dressage?" Stevie asked as they turned into the park and Dorothy flashed her pass at the man at the gate. "I mean, will Southwood?"

"I think so," Dorothy said. "You never know—something could happen to upset him. But I don't think it will."

IT DIDN'T. WHEN Southwood entered the arena, The Saddle Club could see from their seats in the grandstand that he was relaxed and focusing on Nigel's commands. The two moved in partnership from their opening halt to their final salute.

"It's not just that Southwood trots when he should be trotting," Stevie said, watching the test intently. "It's the way he trots. Do you see how all his power seems to come from his back legs? Do you see how his head just seems to flow into Nigel's hands?"

Carole and Lisa exchanged amused glances. Stevie, who was normally animated and disorganized, loved the rhythms and precision of dressage.

Lisa watched Nigel turn Southwood into a tight canter circle. Southwood's body was bent from his nose to his tail—Lisa knew that was difficult for a horse to do. "I wish they'd do a *piaffe* in this test," she said. A *piaffe* was a strong, powerful trot done entirely in place—much more difficult, and more beautiful, than it sounded. Lisa had seen it only in photographs.

Stevie shook her head. "They never would, not in a three-day event, not even in the Olympics," she said. "It's much too difficult a move. Only horses that are dressage specialists do it."

Carole nodded. "Event horses do dressage and show jumping, but you could say they specialize in cross-country," she explained to Lisa. "The dressage and show jumping the eventers do is easier than the stuff international dressage riders and show jumpers do."

"I didn't know there were international show jumpers," Lisa replied. She frowned. Even though she wasn't as experienced as her friends, she wanted to know as much about riding as they did.

"Sure," Carole said. "There are really three Olympic equestrian teams from each country—one for eventing, one for dressage, and one for show jumping."

"I get it," said Lisa. "And Nigel's trying out for the eventing team."

"Shhh!" whispered Stevie. They watched closely as Nigel and Southwood finished their test. At the end, Nigel halted Southwood in the exact center of the arena, doffed his hat to the judges, then let the reins slide long through his fingers. Southwood stretched his neck almost to the ground as he walked out of the ring.

"That was beautiful," Stevie said dreamily.

Carole and Lisa agreed. They'd watched enough of the earlier riders to know that Southwood's test was well above average. He had started off well.

"Of course," Lisa said thoughtfully, "Nigel doesn't have any reason to hold Southwood back during his dressage test. Southwood knows all the movements, he's just judged on how well he does them. It's only during the cross-country that Nigel wants to ease up."

"Right," said Carole. "And it's cross-country that will count the most to the people choosing the Olympic event teams."

Stevie sighed. "We still haven't done anything to convince Nigel to give Southwood a chance. I've made a lot of little comments, but we haven't done anything big."

"We've all made a lot of little comments," Lisa remarked, "and I think they're sliding right off Nigel's back. But I don't know how to convince him—and I keep

67

thinking that, after all, he does know more about this than we do."

Suddenly Carole sat up straight and elbowed her two friends. "Look!"

On the edge of the crowd, at the foot of the grandstand, Drew was scanning the spectators. When he caught sight of The Saddle Club, he waved. Then he turned and spoke to a shorter boy next to him, who was facing the arena. The boy had his back to the grandstand.

"It's Eddy!" Stevie whispered. "Run!" They got up and scrambled down from the stands.

"Pretend you don't see them," Lisa said. "Act normal. Act like we're going to go congratulate Nigel."

Carole peeked over her shoulder. "Here they come!"

The Saddle Club dashed through the crowd. "Where do we go now?" Carole asked when they were safely away from the grandstand.

"Why, girls—what a happy coincidence!" Mrs. Harrington had been walking down the road. When she saw them she stopped and smiled. "Do you have plans for the rest of the afternoon?" she said. "Because I happen to be free—I'm just going home now—and I did promise you a tour of Blue Hill."

The Saddle Club jumped at the chance. The past two nights they'd stayed so late at Rolex that it had been dark when they sat down to dinner in the Blue Hill dining room. They had been through most of the house, but they still hadn't seen the rest of the farm. They dashed back to the stables and found Dorothy to tell her where they were going, then rode in Mrs. Harrington's car back to Blue Hill.

Blue Hill was enchanting. Mrs. Harrington showed them the stallion barn, where four Thoroughbred stallions lived in equine luxury. Each had its own private pasture adjoining a large, clean stall. "Don't try to pet them," Mrs. Harrington warned the girls. "They're strong-minded animals, and you have to be careful around them. I don't allow Drake or Tory into this barn."

"We know not to pet them," Carole said. They looked at the stallions with respect.

Next Mrs. Harrington led them through the two large broodmare barns. The stalls were extralarge, for safe foaling, and each one was equipped with a tiny video camera.

"You videotape the horses being born?" Stevie asked in astonishment.

Mrs. Harrington laughed. "The cameras are hooked up to a closed-circuit TV monitor," she explained. "We have so many mares here that during foaling season we sometimes have several giving birth at once. We use the monitor so that it takes only one person to watch for the time when the horses go into labor."

Most of the stalls were empty because most of the

mares had already had their babies and were grazing with the foals in the pastures. Mrs. Harrington walked them past several pastures, and they stopped to admire the baby horses frolicking. "They're adorable!" Carole said. "We have a young horse named Samson at Pine Hollow. We helped with his birth and a lot of his training."

"We'll sell most of these babies as yearlings in the fall," Mrs. Harrington said. "They'll be trained elsewhere. Then, next spring—more foals."

"It must be lovely to have so many babies around," Carole said, "but hard to let them go."

"It is," Mrs. Harrington admitted. "However, we certainly couldn't keep them all. Come, let's introduce you to the riding horses."

In a small, tidy stable close to the main house lived three horses and two ponies. Mrs. Harrington owned a black mare named Jenny. "She's my field hunter," Mrs. Harrington explained. "Bennett here belongs to Mr. Harrington, and each of us rides Trilby sometimes."

The children's two ponies were named Amazing Grace and Sam. "You have to call her *Amazing* Grace," Mrs. Harrington said. "Not just Grace. Tory is quite firm about that." She gave the palomino pony a loving pat. Sam was a slightly sturdier chestnut. He happily crunched the carrot that Carole offered him.

Mrs. Harrington checked her watch. "The children

70

will be home from school soon," she said. "Do say something nice about the ponies to them. They're so impressed with the three of you, ever since Dorothy told them how well you ride, that I know praise from you would mean a lot."

"It won't be hard to say something nice about these ponies," Carole said. "They're really sweet, and they're good-looking, too." She looked around the little stable. "All of your horses are super high quality," she said frankly.

"Nothing like our renegade," Lisa said. Seeing how well all the Blue Hill horses lived had made her think sadly about poor Ghost. She couldn't get him out of her mind. She knew that Ghost couldn't stay in the horse hospital forever, and she really wanted him to have a good home.

"I don't know," Carole said thoughtfully. "Ghost had good conformation underneath all those scars, and Dr. Lawrence said he was a Thoroughbred. I bet that in his good years he looked as handsome as these horses."

"Who's Ghost?" Mrs. Harrington asked. The Saddle Club realized that they hadn't told her about their rescue of the day before. They'd described Ghost to Dorothy and Nigel on the ride back to Blue Hill from Rolex, but at dinner the conversation had centered around Nigel's dressage test and then had turned to other competitors

71

and their chances at Rolex. The Saddle Club had found everything so absorbing that they hadn't mentioned Ghost to the Harringtons. Now they told Mrs. Harrington the story.

"He really needs a good home," Carole finished, "if you would happen to know anyone with lots of land—" She stopped suddenly and blushed. Mrs. Harrington had lots of land, but Carole hadn't meant to imply that she should take Ghost.

On the other hand, it would be a perfect solution . . . but how could they ask Mrs. Harrington for such a big favor? Carole knew that even horses in retirement needed to have veterinary care. They needed to have their hooves trimmed, and they probably needed grain and a blanket in the winter. All that could be expensive.

Lisa and Stevie knew exactly what Carole was thinking. "We mean," Lisa said, "if you knew someone who maybe didn't need so much pasture—"

"Someone who wanted another horse around," Stevie said.

"He's very friendly," Carole said. She tried not to shuffle her feet.

Mrs. Harrington laughed, then looked serious. "Girls," she said, "another horse around here wouldn't make a dent in the grass. I wouldn't mind giving your Ghost a home, but I can't promise you anything. Horses, espe-

72

cially ones that have been mistreated, can carry diseases with them for a long time. If Ghost brought a strange virus to Blue Hill, our foals could all become seriously ill. I can't allow that."

She sighed. "I'll talk to Mr. Harrington tonight," she offered. "If he agrees, I'll come meet Ghost and speak to the veterinarian. Then, if we can find a suitable place for Ghost to live in quarantine for a few months—away from other horses—then maybe he can live here. It's the best I can do. Okay?"

"Of course," Lisa said. She understood Mrs. Harrington's reasoning—none of them would ever want to endanger the beautiful foals! "It's very nice of you. It means so much to us."

"I can tell," Mrs. Harrington said kindly.

"He's such a nice horse," Lisa continued. "I'm sure you'll like him."

"I'm sure I will."

They walked quietly back to the house. *It's a lot of "ifs,"* Stevie thought. *If Mr. Harrington agrees, if Ghost is healthy, if we can find a quarantine . . .* Yet she knew Mrs. Harrington's offer was generous. *I only wish we could do something to repay her. Not only might she save Ghost, but she rescued us from Dready Eddy for yet another day.*

73

"STEADY, STEADY! EASY, Southwood! Whoa!" Drew led Southwood out of the stables on Friday morning. It was a rest day for Southwood, since the other half of the Rolex field was riding their dressage tests that day. Southwood, however, looked anything but restful: He snorted and plunged and tossed his head. When Nigel mounted him, Southwood gave a quick buck before snatching at the bit and taking off at a trot.

Nigel waved gaily to The Saddle Club and Dorothy as he rode away. "We'll just take a little walk around the park," he called. Southwood tossed his head again and

74

kicked out at a scrap of paper. "Whoa, old boy!" Nigel turned his full attention to the horse.

The Saddle Club was astonished. Yesterday Southwood had been calm and businesslike, and today he looked like a rocket ship ready to blast off. They hadn't known he could act so wild, and Lisa found it alarming. Dorothy, however, was laughing. "Southwood's turned into a true event horse," she said. "He really hasn't been in very many three-day events, but already he knows he's supposed to do cross-country the day after dressage. Southwood's ready to go."

Drew shaded his hand with his eyes and continued to watch Nigel and Southwood. "Just like Prospero," he said, a wistful look on his face. "He loved eventing, and he especially loved cross-country. He was a big, handsome, dark dappled gray, Lisa, and when he was about to start cross-country he would arch his neck and whinny." Drew looked sad. "He was so beautiful!"

"Ghost, the horse we found on Tuesday, acted a little like that," Lisa said. They'd told Drew about the rescue and Mrs. Harrington's kindness. "He seemed to want to be at Rolex. It was almost as if he knew what was going on."

"Dr. Lawrence said maybe Ghost was an old show horse," Stevie added. "He thought Ghost saw all the people and horses and wanted to be at the show."

"You never know," Dorothy said, to The Saddle Club's surprise, because they found Dr. Lawrence's idea a little far-fetched. "Horses have strange memories. Sometimes they forget things right away, and sometimes they never, ever do. I once had a mare who was almost run over by a mailman. Great big trucks, strange tractors, and noisy motorcycles never scared her, but from the day the mailman nearly hit her, she became terrified of Jeeps, because they looked like mail trucks. She never lost that fear."

"Prospero wasn't afraid of anything," Drew said.

Friday was the first day that there were more spectators at Rolex than people riding or helping out. "Did you notice that the trade fair is open today?" Dorothy asked The Saddle Club as Drew went back into the stables to clean Southwood's stall.

"I saw a candied apple stand when we were driving in," Stevie said.

"Right between the show-jumping ring and the main park buildings," Dorothy said, nodding her head. "That's it. There's a circle of food vendors, a big tent, and a lot of little tents. Everything that's for sale—except for the food—has something to do with horses."

Carole's eyes lit up. "That sounds fun," she said. Maybe she could find something special for Starlight.

"I could really go for a candied apple," Stevie added.

"Let's all go!" Lisa said. "You, too, Dorothy—Nigel won't be back for a while."

Dorothy shook her head. "I have a few things to do for Nigel," she admitted. "You girls go ahead. But why don't you wait for Eddy? Drew said he'd be here any minute, and he's hardly seen you all week."

Lisa didn't know what to say. Eddy hadn't seen them *once* all week, and they hadn't seen him. Operation Duck Dready Eddy had been a roaring success.

"I *really* need a candied apple," Stevie said. "I'm going to get sick if I don't eat something soon." She clutched her stomach and tried to look faint.

Dorothy smiled but shook her head. "Eddy is a really sweet boy," she said. "I think you girls would like him."

"I know we would," Carole said, "but I don't think we should wait if it means making Stevie sick." She took her friend's arm solicitously. "Come on, Stevie. We'll take care of you."

Dorothy rolled her eyes and laughed as they walked away, Lisa and Carole clutching a staggering Stevie. "I think she's on to us," Lisa said. "She knows we're avoiding Eddy."

"Well, we haven't exactly been subtle about it, have we?" Carole asked. "Stevie, I think you can walk normally now. Dorothy isn't looking."

"Good," Stevie said. She walked faster. "I do want a

candied apple, and maybe some onion rings to go with it."
She glanced at her friends. "We're being as subtle as we
can," she said at last.

"Which means not very subtle," said Lisa. "It's hard to
be subtle and stay away from Eddy."

Stevie grinned. "You want to bring him along to the
fair?"

"No. I really don't. Every time Dorothy calls him sweet,
I remember my mother telling me how much I'd love my
'really sweet' cousin Larry. He came to spend a week with
us when I was seven." Lisa shuddered. "He had a rock
collection! All week long he dug around the sidewalk,
looking for 'specimens.' Weird!"

"Rocks don't make me think about Eddy," Carole said.
"They make me think of Simon Atherton." This time
they all shuddered.

"Doesn't Simon collect stamps?" Stevie asked.

Simon was a geeky boy who rode at Pine Hollow. Lisa
knew she didn't want to spend time around him. She was
glad they'd stayed away from Eddy.

The fair was terrific. Stevie got her candied apple and
onion rings, Lisa had pork barbecue, and Carole ate an
Italian sausage. They all had lemonade. Then they wan-
dered through the tents, admiring breeches, horse books,
new types of horse fencing, boots, brushes, show halters,
and more.

78

"You could buy everything for a horse here except the horse," Carole said admiringly. After some thought, she picked out a new soft face brush for Starlight. Lisa bought a hot pink nylon halter with green hearts on it, and Stevie tried on a pair of riding tights that had neon horses galloping down the seams. They walked through the display of new horse trailers and sat on some new saddles. Finally they all bought matching "Kentucky Rolex Three-Day Event" sweatshirts.

When they walked back to the stables wearing their new sweatshirts, Drew said, "Here comes the terrible trio," and gave them a grin. Nigel had just dismounted and was loosening the girth on Southwood's saddle. Nigel's hair was wet with sweat beneath his hard hat, and he looked a little ruffled. Southwood had his ears back.

"Eddy's just gone off to the trailer," Drew said. "He'll be back in a minute if you girls—" He broke off when Nigel motioned for his help. Southwood didn't seem to want his saddle removed. Nigel lifted it from his back while Drew held Southwood steady, murmuring, "Easy, boy, easy."

"Whew!" Nigel slicked his damp hair back from his forehead as Drew led Southwood into the barn. "That was a bit of an invigorating ride." He dropped onto a straw bale that was sitting outside the stables. Earlier Carole had seen a woman use it as a mounting block to get onto her very tall horse.

"Perhaps we'll just go back to the fair," Stevie said, making vague motions to Carole with her hands.

"You *know*," Lisa said, adding emphasis to Stevie's motions. Eddy was on his way!

"Just a minute," Carole said. "I wanted to ask Nigel something."

"Shoot," Nigel said, looking up from his seat on the bale.

"Is Southwood a good show jumper? And what makes a good show jumper, anyway?" Carole, who loved show jumping, had been wondering about this ever since she'd seen Southwood's elegant dressage test and his enthusiasm for cross-country.

"The answer to your first question is yes," Nigel said. "As for your second, a good show jumper needs to be able to shorten and lengthen his strides so that he can take off from a good spot in front of the fence. He needs to be agile so that he can land, turn, and jump quickly." Nigel smiled. "Most importantly, he needs to not want to knock the fences down."

"Not want to knock them down?" Stevie repeated, intrigued despite her desire to get out of Eddy territory. "You mean he wants to leave them up?"

"That's right," Nigel answered. "Show jumping is one

phase where some event horses have an almost critical failing. They never hit the solid fences on cross-country day, but it doesn't seem to bother them when they hit the flimsy show-jumping rails." He laughed. "Wait till Sunday and you'll see. I happen to know that one horse here is exactly like that. He'll probably do well on cross-country, but he'll be lucky if he hits less than half a dozen jumps on the show-jumping course. He makes a mess!"

"I didn't think three-day event show jumping was supposed to be all that hard," Carole said. "The fences aren't as big as the cross-country ones." She had always been told that the true purpose of the show-jumping phase in an event was to prove that the horse still had stamina left after cross-country day.

"That's what I mean," Nigel said. "In many cases, event horses that do poorly at show jumping aren't bad jumpers or even tired, they just aren't bothering to be careful. Good show jumpers need to be careful all the time."

They watched a horse leave the stables. This one, like Southwood, was full of energy and ready to go. "How about Southwood?" Lisa asked. "Is he careful?"

Nigel laughed. "Very," he said. "He seems upset whenever he touches a rail, even if it doesn't fall down. He really loves to jump, too."

"Does he get tired?" Carole asked.

Nigel shook his head. "I know how to get him in good shape and keep him there, but beyond that, Southwood's really an exceptional athlete. You know, he's never had a single fault in show jumping—never a single rail down."

Carole thought about this. To Carole, Southwood sounded—and looked—like a natural. "I don't understand," she said quietly.

"Meaning," Nigel asked, "that you still don't understand why I'm not trying for the Olympics?"

All three of the girls nodded. Nigel sighed. "I know it's hard for you to understand," he said. "It's a tough decision to make. I think, though, that I'm making the right choice in saving Southwood for future events. Southwood is only seven years old. That's the minimum age a horse can be and still compete internationally. Because he's so young, he hasn't gotten much exposure to difficult events. The fences here are going to be a step up for him. The Olympic course will be even harder. Like I told you earlier, I do want Southwood to have a chance at the Olympics—just not this Olympics."

"I know you'll do what you think is best," Carole said, "and I know you know what you're doing, so I can't argue with you. It's just that we want Southwood to have a chance, too. Drew says that his Prospero never got a chance. And I keep thinking that Ghost, the horse we rescued the other day, maybe never got a chance, either."

Nigel nodded. "I want Southwood to have a chance, too," he repeated. "How is Ghost?"

"The trail guide had said that maybe she could find him a home," Lisa reported. "But today she said that she couldn't after all. Her friends with a farm don't have room for another horse."

"We went back to the hospital this morning," Stevie said. "Ghost looks great, but Dr. Lawrence says he can't keep him there much longer. They've gotten in three more horses that are really sick, and they need the space."

Carole sighed. "Dr. Lawrence is going to bring Ghost here in a trailer this afternoon so that Mrs. Harrington can see him when she's done with her meeting. If we can find a place for quarantine, Ghost might be able to go to Blue Hill."

Nigel nodded. "Quarantine can be hard to arrange," he said. "Dorothy and I will do what we can, and you girls keep looking, too. All horses deserve good homes. They can't all be superstars, but they all deserve love and care."

The girls nodded. They couldn't agree more.

Nigel looked into the crowd. "Here comes Drew!" he said pleasantly.

"Run!" Stevie whispered. "It's Eddy!"

"DUCK! THERE HE IS!" The Saddle Club crouched behind a parked car. It was late afternoon. After successfully dodging Eddy that morning, they'd returned to the stables only to find him and Drew lying in wait.

They weren't actually lying, thought Lisa. They were playing cards on the same bale of straw that Carole and Nigel had sat on earlier. Eddy's back was to them.

"He's got blond hair," Lisa said. "I didn't know that. I thought it would be that funny mouse color, like Drew's."

"I wish we could see his face," Carole whispered.

"We're about to," Stevie said gloomily. "Mrs. Harrington and Dr. Lawrence will be here any minute, and it

84

doesn't look like Drew and Eddy are going to move." She shrugged her shoulders. "We fought a good fight," she said.

"We've been lucky," Carole said resignedly. "I didn't think we'd be able to go this long."

Lisa's eyes lit up with an expression of mischief more usually seen on Stevie's face. "Stevie, I'm disappointed in you!" she said to her friend. "I've got the greatest idea! Wait here!"

Carole and Stevie watched as Lisa dashed toward the tents. "*She's* got an idea?" mumbled Stevie.

In a few minutes they heard the show PA system crackle to life. "Would Mr. Edwin Gustafs please report to the business office," a voice droned through the speakers. "Ed Gustafs, to the business office."

Stevie's jaw dropped. "Why didn't I think of that?"

Carole was laughing so hard that she had to sit down on the ground. "I can't believe she did that! And look— it's working!" They watched as Eddy got up and shuffled off. Drew gathered the cards and went into the stable.

Lisa came running back. "How was that?" she asked.

"Success!" They gave each other a high fifteen. "And not any too soon," added Carole. "Here's Dr. Lawrence."

A battered old trailer pulled up next to the stable entrance. The Saddle Club ran to open the back door and let down the ramp, and Dr. Lawrence gently led Ghost out.

As the horse walked down the ramp with his elegant head held high, Stevie felt a shudder go through her. He looked more like a Ghost than ever—a ghost of a truly great horse. Despite his scarred legs, his unkempt coat, and his scrawny body, Ghost stepped out as though he were a champion in his prime. He looked as though he expected to find himself in the stabling area of Kentucky Rolex. He looked as though he belonged there.

Mrs. Harrington pulled up in her white four-wheel-drive. She got out with a smile for The Saddle Club and Dr. Lawrence and walked up to Ghost, holding out her hand. "My," she said, "isn't he a handsome animal?"

Drew came out of the stable, whistling.

Ghost turned his head toward the sound. He stood transfixed for a long moment. Then he took a deep breath and let it out in a long, shuddering whinny. Drew looked up, startled, and stared at the tall, regal horse. His eyes widened and his mouth dropped open. "Is it you?" Drew whispered. He took one hesitant step toward the horse, then another. "Prospero?" Drew uttered increduously. Then louder, "Prospero?"

Ghost carefully lifted his hoof in the air and offered it to Drew.

"Prospero!"

Drew's cry was part joy, part anguish. He launched himself at Ghost. He threw his arms around the horse's neck. Tears streamed down his face. Ghost turned his head gently and nuzzled Drew's sleeve, still waving his hoof in the air. Drew patted him, choking back sobs. "Oh, Prospero, you good boy," he said, bending down to shake his hoof. "I don't even have a carrot."

The Saddle Club stood still, shocked and amazed. "Our Ghost is *Prospero?*" Lisa whispered.

"Drew?" Nigel rushed out of the stables. "Are you okay?" He slowed when he saw Drew hugging the gray-white horse, then stopped. He stared at Ghost—or at Prospero.

"It's him!" Drew was laughing now. "It's really him! I'd know him anywhere. And he knew me!"

Nigel walked forward and looked at the horse from the side. "It's him, all right," he said. He stroked Prospero's neck and ran his hand down one of his scarred legs, then straightened and gave the horse a hearty pat. Even Nigel's eyes shone with tears.

Mrs. Harrington took a handkerchief out of her pocket and dabbed her eyes. Then she rummaged in the back of her car and returned with a bag of carrots. "Here," she said, handing them to Drew. "Who is he?"

87

"His name's Prospero," Drew said. He fed Prospero carrot after carrot. "He's the best horse. Oh, look at him, look at his legs. Oh, buddy, what's happened to you?"

"He's all right now," Dr. Lawrence said. "He'll never be comfortable running or jumping, but he could be ridden quietly."

"He looks so different," Drew said, "and yet I knew him the instant I saw him. His coat's gone white, of course, because he's so much older, and his face is thinner, but it's still the same face—the same kind, regal face. I knew I'd never forget what he looked like. Look, Nigel"—Drew felt the underside of Prospero's chin—"remember when that branch cut him and he had to have stitches? Here's the scar, right under his noseband."

"He's your horse, all right," Nigel said. "I've never forgotten him, either."

Drew stepped back from Prospero to look at him fully, and his smile dissolved. "How could I let this happen to him?" he said. "I love him so—how could I let him get like this?" His happy tears had dried, but now he looked ready to cry from sorrow.

Lisa came forward and gave Prospero a pat. "You told me he was capable of more than you could do," she said to Drew. "You told me you wanted him to have a rider who could take him to the top."

Drew nodded.

Carole, catching Lisa's argument, added, "And you sold him to a good person, and a good rider."

Drew nodded again.

"Didn't you tell us that he hurt himself while he was in his pasture?" Stevie asked.

"He hurt his tendon," Drew said. "He was running, and he tripped."

"That would have happened no matter who owned him," Lisa said firmly. "Accidents can happen to any horse anytime, just like they can happen to any person. You sold him to a good home for a good reason. What happened after isn't your fault."

Drew looked at The Saddle Club and smiled. "You're right, I know," he said. "Thanks."

"Besides," Nigel said, "you'll be able to take care of him from now on."

Drew's face shone with gratitude and happiness. "I could never, ever, leave him again," he said.

"You won't have to," Nigel promised him. "There's plenty of room for him at our farm. We don't have any foals to worry about. He can come home in the trailer with Southwood."

"Home," Drew repeated.

Mrs. Harrington smiled. "Not a ghost after all," she

said. "What a lovely day." She promised to see them all soon at Blue Hill and prepared to get back into her car, but Drew stopped her.

"Thank you," he said. "The girls told me you were considering giving him a home." Drew thanked Dr. Lawrence, too, for rescuing Prospero and nursing him back to health. Then he thanked The Saddle Club.

"We didn't do that much," Carole said. "Of course we couldn't let him run loose through the horse park. All we did was catch him and take him back to the hospital."

"And try to find him a home, and arrange for him to come here," Drew continued.

"But that was an accident," Stevie protested. "That was just luck."

"You did a lot, and I'll always be grateful," Drew said firmly. He put his arm across Prospero's withers. "You're right, it was luck. He's always been a great horse, and now he's a lucky one, too."

THAT NIGHT THEY ate dinner at a pizza parlor in Lexington. Nigel ordered a superlarge thick-crust pizza with everything, but when it arrived he hardly nibbled on one slice.

"Ummm—looks good!" Carole said, even though she hated anchovies and couldn't believe Nigel had ordered them. "Here, Stevie," she added, picking through the toppings on her slice, "you can have my anchovies."

"Only if you take my olives," Stevie muttered. "I hate olives."

"I don't know why you two are so picky," Lisa said cheerfully. "This looks wonderful!" She took a big bite, chewed, choked, and turned red. She swallowed hard and gulped some water. "So that's what anchovies taste like," she said. "I never had them before."

"I'll show you what they look like," Carole offered. "That way you can pick them off your pizza."

While they were poring over Lisa's slice of pizza, Stevie looked at Nigel. He was sipping his iced tea with a tight, thoughtful expression on his face. He still hadn't eaten anything.

"I wonder how Prospero is," Stevie said. Since noncompeting horses weren't allowed to stay in the Kentucky Rolex stables, Drew and Eddy had taken Prospero back to the horse hospital for the weekend. Drew and Eddy were there now, making sure Prospero was comfortable. Stevie knew that Prospero would be comfortable. She also knew that Drew just wanted to stay with Prospero. She didn't blame him. Somehow, they still hadn't been forced to meet Dready Eddy.

"He's wonderful," Carole said. "He's happy."

Nigel pushed his plate away. Dorothy gave him a sympathetic look but didn't say anything. The Saddle Club didn't say anything, either. They all understood the enormous test that Nigel and Southwood were going to face the next morning on the cross-country course. Even the easy routes over the fences were fantastically difficult. No wonder Nigel seemed so nervous.

THAT EVENING AFTER dinner Dorothy and Nigel wanted to return to the Rolex stables to finish getting Southwood ready for the morning. They offered to take the girls back to Blue Hill. "We'd rather wander around the horse park," Carole said. "No one will care, will they?"

"Just stick to open areas," Nigel said. "We'll be ready to leave in an hour."

"Let's go back to the hospital," Carole suggested, after they had walked past the start box and the first few fences, all set and ready for the morning. "Let's just look in on Prospero."

"Eddy," Lisa objected.

"We wouldn't have to go into the stable," Carole said. "We could just peek in and be sure he's okay. I mean, I know he is," she added, "I just want to look at him. I don't know why. I'm so amazed that Ghost is really him."

Stevie checked her watch. "We'll have to hurry." They

walked quickly across the park. The setting sun shone golden on the grass. They reached the hospital grounds and walked to the stable where Prospero was staying. The large main door was open a crack. Stevie peeked inside, then jumped back.

"Duck!" she whispered.

"Is it Eddy?" asked Lisa.

"No! It's Nigel!"

"Nigel?" Lisa asked. She and Carole peered inside. Prospero stood in his usual stall, his head over the half door. Nigel stood alone in front of the old gray-white horse. His hands were on his hips, and he appeared to be talking quietly and earnestly.

"Who's he talking to?" Stevie whispered. She'd come forward again and joined Carole and Lisa at the door. Nigel didn't notice them.

"Prospero, I guess," Lisa said.

"Why?" asked Stevie. None of them knew the answer. Nigel quit talking. He and Prospero stood silently, regarding each other. Nigel put his hand out to stroke the horse.

"Nigel!" a voice shouted from the other end of the stable. "How much grain do you think he should have?"

"Drew and Eddy!" Carole whispered. The girls scampered away. Soon they were back on the park grounds.

"Prospero looked good," Stevie said. "But what was

Nigel doing there? He knew Drew could take care of his own horse."

"He was talking to Prospero," Carole said. "He looked really thoughtful, didn't he? He looked that way at dinner, too. I thought he was nervous, but maybe he wasn't."

The girls stopped and looked at each other. "Maybe he's thinking about how Prospero never got a chance to be a great competitor," Stevie said.

"And maybe he's thinking about Southwood's chances to be one," Carole added.

Lisa asked, "Do you think Nigel could be changing his mind?"

The girls let the question hang in the air, unanswered.

CROSS-COUNTRY DAY dawned warm and clear. Once again Nigel and Dorothy went to the horse park before The Saddle Club was even awake, but the girls woke early, too. They ate a quick breakfast with Mrs. Harrington in the quiet kitchen at Blue Hill, then helped Mrs. Harrington load her mare Jenny into a horse trailer. Even Jenny seemed impatient to get to Rolex. She whinnied and shook and stamped her feet.

The first thing they noticed as they approached the horse park was the steady line of cars flowing into the parking lot. "Wow!" Stevie said. "Look at all the people!"

Mrs. Harrington smiled. "You didn't expect it? After

95

all, this is the biggest event in America, and today's the most exciting day. People come from all over to see it."

"They'll all be watching Nigel," Lisa said thoughtfully.

Stevie laughed. "I bet he won't be watching them!"

"Probably not," Carole agreed. "Anyway, it's Southwood that people will want to see." Carole sighed, and all the members of The Saddle Club thought about last night's quiet dinner and about seeing Nigel with Prospero afterward. They'd agreed not to say anything to Nigel about it.

Mrs. Harrington turned her truck into a side entrance of the park and stopped in an area reserved for the outriders. The girls helped her unload Jenny before hurrying to the stabling area.

The place was a mess—people were everywhere! Lisa thought she'd never seen such orderly chaos. Though it looked like everyone knew exactly what he or she ought to be doing, everyone was doing it as fast as possible, and the horses, riders, and grooms all seemed excited and intense.

"It's overwhelming," Carole whispered. The others nodded. They tried to stay out of everyone's way. They didn't see Nigel, Dorothy, Southwood, or even Drew.

"I'd almost welcome Dready Eddy," Stevie said. "At least he could tell us whether Nigel's already left. What if he has!"

"He couldn't have." Lisa opened her dog-eared program. "See? Nigel starts his roads-and-tracks—that's the warm-up trot—in fifteen minutes. Then he goes straight on to cross-country. It's all timed so that the riders start cross-country five minutes apart."

"Could he be down by the start line already?" Carole peered anxiously through the crowd. She knew there was not much they could do to help Southwood before he started, but she wanted just one glimpse of him to see how he looked before he began. To see if he looked like a champion, a true gold medal horse.

"No—there he is!" Stevie jumped up and down and waved at Dorothy. The girls went quickly to Southwood's side.

This is what a champion looks like, Carole thought. Southwood seemed about to burst from energy, yet he stood still while Nigel tightened the saddle girth, breathing deeply, eyes alert, muscles quivering. He knew it was cross-country day, and he was ready to run.

Nigel, too, had lost his nervous look. He seemed intent, almost grim, as he made a last-minute check of Southwood's tack; but as he snapped his stirrups into position, he caught Stevie's eye and winked. Stevie, astonished, burst out laughing. "We were worried about you!" she said.

"Sorry," Nigel said with a quick grin. "I've had a lot to

think about. I'm fine, don't worry, and so's Southwood."
He vaulted easily into the saddle and laid a hand on
Southwood's sweating shoulder. "I'm very glad you girls
came with us this week," he said before he rode away.

"Gosh!" Lisa said. "Imagine him thinking to say that at
a time like this!"

Dorothy folded Southwood's cooling sheet in her arms.
"He's right," she said. "We're both glad you came. And to
answer the question I know you're about to ask, no, you
can't do anything to help us now. Drew's gathering the
stuff Southwood will need at the start box, and Eddy's
going to help us carry it there. This is a really big course,
and if you three want to see Southwood over any of the
fences you'd better start walking. It'll take you a while to
get there."

Stevie could see that Carole was about to protest and
say they should help Southwood at the start. "Eddy," she
whispered warningly.

"Okay," Carole said to Dorothy instead. "If you're
sure."

"I'm sure."

Since they had walked the course with Nigel, they believed they already knew where the most interesting
jumps were. Unfortunately, the most interesting jumps
weren't anywhere near one another, nor were they near
the start or finish lines. Lisa opened her program to the

course map and they took one last look at it, even though they had already discussed what they were going to do.

"Here, here, and here," Lisa said, pointing. "We'll meet at the finish." The Saddle Club split up.

CAROLE TOOK UP a position near the Lexington Bank. This was a giant man-made hill, covered with grass, rising out of the rolling horse park terrain. From her vantage point, Carole could see three sides of the bank. If Nigel took the long route, as she knew he'd planned, he would turn to the side of the bank, go over a rail fence, jump Southwood up a series of small steps carved into the bank, jump a fence at the top, turn again to jump down over an enormous drop fence, and then sail over an arrowhead fence on his way out. The short route took the horses straight up two really giant steps, then over the top fence, and headlong over the big drop. The big steps were close enough to the top fence that the horses didn't have much time to pull themselves together.

Over the PA system, which could be heard across the entire park, Carole heard the announcer say, "Southwood and Nigel Hawthorne, now on course." She felt her heart beat faster.

The horse just before Southwood came galloping toward the bank. Carole could see him from far away; as he galloped closer, the fence attendant, mounted on a horse, blew a sharp whistle. The crowd stilled and pressed against the ropes outlining the course. Carole drew in her breath.

The rider, a woman wearing a blue jersey and a white helmet, pointed her horse at the quick route. Up, up! Carole had never seen a horse jump such a steep bank before. The horse did well, but as it reached the top it seemed to lose energy and impulsion. It looked at the narrow top fence and stopped. There was not much the rider could do. She circled the horse in the tiny space and gave it an encouraging tap with her crop, and the horse gathered itself and jumped over and then down the drop. "Good boy!" the rider shouted as they cleared the arrowhead and continued on.

"Does that count against them?" Carole asked a woman standing next to her. After all, the horse had jumped correctly on the second try.

"Twenty penalty points," the woman answered. "It should put them out of contention."

Just for a little error like that? Carole shivered. She began to understand why Nigel would choose the long routes. Did Southwood have a chance?

Here they came! The fence attendant blew her whistle. Carole watched Nigel and Southwood approach the fence. "Go, Southwood!" she shouted. "Go, Nigel!"

Nigel was concentrating so hard that Carole knew he

would never hear her. Southwood looked equally intense. Carole had never seen a horse look so fierce, so intent upon jumping.

She held her breath. In the final few strides before the bank, Carole waited for Nigel to turn Southwood for the easier jumps to the side. Instead, Nigel seemed to draw in his own breath. He put his legs on Southwood and steered him straight for the short route!

Up, up, two strides, over, and down! Where the previous horse had faltered, Southwood kept steady, and Nigel drove him forward. Straight, fast, and clean! Carole cheered as they galloped away. Why had they taken the short route? Carole caught her breath. Lisa's guess must be correct! Nigel was going for gold!

"SOUTHWOOD FAST AND CLEAR over the Lexington Bank!" Stevie heard the announcer and screamed in jubilation. She realized what the words "fast and clear" meant— Southwood had taken the short route and he'd made it.

Stevie was standing near the lake. She knew this was one of the complexes that Nigel was most worried about. For the short route the horses had to jump two almost-four-foot-high fences in a row, without even a stride between them, and land in water, which many horses hated. Just in the time she'd been standing there, Stevie had seen one horse refuse to enter the water and another jump in clumsily and give its rider a dunking. The long route, though, was very long—the horses had to trot and turn, trot and turn, before the jumps. Nigel had told Stevie that time lost here would be very hard to make up later in the course.

Here came Nigel. From far away, Stevie could see him start to slow Southwood. Southwood, however, saw the fence and plunged forward eagerly.

"Let him try it, Nigel!" Stevie said, even though she knew Nigel couldn't hear. He hesitated, then shifted Southwood back on-course for the bounce into the water. Stevie felt her heart almost stop. What if Southwood *couldn't* do it?

Other horses might have been put off by the water, but not Southwood. He jumped the first fence, jumped the second, and *splash!* Southwood stumbled as he landed. Nigel fought for balance, grabbing Southwood's mane. Just in front of them was a jump that was actually in the water—a bank like an island, with a fence on top. Southwood floundered, fighting to get his feet back under him. Water flew up around them.

Nigel could have stopped Southwood, turned him, and taken a slower, easier approach to the island. Instead he sat steady, giving the horse his head so that he could regain his balance but encouraging him toward the island. "Up!" Nigel said, and Southwood took heart. He pulled

102

himself up, jumped the bank, then made a tremendous effort and cleared the fence that was on it.

"Good *boy*!" Nigel shouted.

"Good *boy*!" Stevie echoed. The crowd cheered. Southwood splashed back into the water, then galloped to dry land with a satisfied swish of his tail. Stevie didn't know who was more amazing—Nigel or Southwood. Nigel wanted to win!

LISA WAS AT the sunken road, a giant square hole with fences on both sides. The fast route went jump, jump, jump, jump—over the fence, into the hole, out, and over. Nigel had said it called for very precise riding. Lisa thought it looked exciting, and a lot of people seemed to agree with her, because there was a big crowd around the fence.

Lisa wiggled her way to the front so that she could see. It had taken her a long time to walk to the jump, and she didn't have long to wait for Southwood. When the fence attendant blew her whistle Lisa looked up—and recognized Mrs. Harrington and Jenny! The crowd pushed against Lisa, trying to see the next horse. "It's Southwood," Lisa heard another spectator say. She leaned closer.

As Nigel and Southwood barreled down the lane from the lake, Lisa caught her breath. It was clear to her that

Nigel wasn't holding Southwood back. He was letting Southwood shine!

Nigel rode Southwood so close to Lisa that she could have caught his stirrup. "Go, go, go," she whispered. Southwood took the short route in textbook fashion, then galloped away to the cheers of the crowd. Lisa thought he looked more Olympic with every stride.

As soon as Southwood was out of sight, Lisa pushed her way through the crowd and ran for the finish line. Southwood had a few more fences to jump, but he'd be traveling at a gallop, and Lisa wanted to see him come in. She had a feeling she'd just witnessed something great.

When Lisa reached the finish, panting for breath, Stevie and Carole were already there, clinging to Dorothy with excitement. Lisa rushed forward to give Dorothy a hug. "Did you see them?" Lisa asked.

"The first few fences," Dorothy said. "But I've been listening to the announcer, too." Her face glowed.

A moment later Southwood came into sight, galloping up a slight rise to the final fence, a large wooden park bench set between two trees. It was big, but, as Nigel had told them, it was meant to be encouragingly easy. Southwood took it in stride, and Nigel galloped him over the finish on loose reins. They had no penalties and no time faults. Southwood's round had been flawless. Nigel's face was aglow with joy.

The girls and Dorothy waited while Nigel removed Southwood's saddle and was weighed out holding it. Then they swarmed over him with congratulations and hugs. "What made you do it, Nigel?" Dorothy asked him. "I could hear that you were taking the risky routes. Why did you change your mind?"

Nigel had one arm around Carole and the other around Southwood. He looked over Dorothy's shoulder at Drew, who had just come running from the course, and smiled. "Prospero," he said. "He never had his chance. I want to make sure that Southwood gets his."

SUDDENLY THERE WAS a lot of work to do. Southwood was covered with sweat and breathing hard, and their first job was to make him comfortable. Dorothy had several buckets of water waiting near the finish, and right away The Saddle Club began to sponge cool water over Southwood's neck and shoulders. Drew removed Southwood's galloping boots and replaced his bridle with a halter and lead rope. Dorothy and Nigel checked every inch of Southwood's body for cuts, scratches, or swellings.

"He looks great," Nigel said with satisfaction. "A little more of that water, girls, then we'll get him walking until he cools off. Lisa, offer him a tiny bit to drink."

106

Drew handed her a different bucket. "I put some salts in it," he said. "It's like horse Gatorade."

Lisa held the bucket under Southwood's nose. "Just a little swallow," she told the horse. She knew too much water could upset a hot horse's stomach. Southwood took a sip, then raised his head and drooled water down the front of Lisa's sweatshirt. He followed that up by rubbing against her. Lisa laughed as she pushed him away. Sweat and horsehair covered her now, but what difference could it make? From running all over the cross-country course, she was already sweaty and muddy. Her jeans were dirty, half of her hair had come out of her ponytail, and her bangs were sticking to her face. Lisa giggled as she picked up an empty water bucket and headed to the pump. She knew her mother would die if she saw her now.

Suddenly someone tapped her on the shoulder. Lisa turned. "This is my brother Eddy," Drew said. "I've been trying to introduce you all week."

Lisa's mouth fell open so fast she was surprised she didn't hear a thud from her chin hitting the ground. Eddy was not mouse-haired, cross-eyed, or goofy. His complexion was as smooth as rose petals. He had high, chiseled cheekbones, beautiful dimples, and perfect blue eyes. He was gorgeous.

In fact, the only thing less than perfect about Eddy's appearance was the look of disappointment on his face.

"I haven't seen you or your friends the whole week," Eddy said. "Have you been hiding from me or something?"

"Uhhh . . ." Lisa became aware that her mouth was still open, and she closed it. Suddenly she wished she weren't covered with horse slime. She wished she weren't sweaty. She wished she weren't dressed like a barn slob. Most of all, she wished she didn't still have chicken-pox marks. She wished she'd met Eddy on the very first day. They could have walked the cross-country course together. "Uh—of course w-we haven't been hiding," she stammered as she filled the bucket at the pump. The truth was, they'd been running away. "We were just busy. But we're not busy now."

"Well, I am." Eddy still looked somewhat disappointed. Lisa couldn't blame him. Of course he knew they'd been avoiding him—no boy was that dumb. "I've got to help Drew," Eddy continued as he and Lisa walked back to Southwood and the others. "I'm sorry I didn't get to know you, Lisa. Drew *said* you were really nice." From his tone, Lisa knew that Eddy didn't think she was necessarily very nice.

Eddy and Drew began walking Southwood back to the stables. Nigel looked at his watch and ran off, still in full riding gear. "He's got to go sign autographs in the *Horse-Play Magazine* booth," Dorothy said. She, Carole, and

108

Stevie were gathering Southwood's gear. Lisa went to help, slinging Southwood's sweaty saddle over her arm. A little more sweat could hardly make a difference at this point.

"You'll never believe it," she groaned. "All week we've been hiding from the most gorgeous boy in the world!" She pointed at Eddy, who was walking beside Drew.

Stevie's and Carole's mouths dropped opened just as Lisa's had. "That's Eddy?" Stevie said. "Wow!"

Dorothy laughed. "I told you that you'd like him," she said. "I knew you girls were avoiding him. Why?"

"It seemed like the thing to do at the time," Carole said lamely, still staring at Eddy.

"Right," Dorothy said, with another laugh and a roll of her eyes. "When I was your age, I might have done the same thing. Fortunately, I grew out of it by the time I met Nigel."

"I think I've grown out of it just now," Lisa said.

LATER THEY ALL went out for a celebratory dinner, Drew and Eddy included. The tension of the night before had been replaced by a general glee. They were all ecstatic over Southwood's success.

"A toast," Nigel said, raising his glass high, "to clean, fast rounds!" They all raised their glasses. Southwood was in sixth place after cross-country. He'd done amazingly well. Nigel drank deeply—he was celebrating with a banana milk shake—and came up with a milky mustache. Dorothy leaned over and playfully wiped it off with her napkin.

"A toast," Stevie said, raising her glass of root beer, "to a real Olympian—and his rider!"

"Now, now," Nigel scolded her, "we still have show jumping tomorrow. Anything could happen." But from the smile on his face The Saddle Club knew he felt confident.

"He's never had a rail down in competition," Carole reminded him.

"And tomorrow would be a bloody awful time to start," Nigel added.

"But you have to admit, things look really good," Lisa said. "There weren't too many clean rounds today—and all of the other British riders had time penalties. You've got a really good shot at the team now." She smiled at Eddy, who was sitting next to her. Or rather, since Eddy had chosen his seat first, she was sitting next to him. Lisa was trying to make up for lost time. "Isn't that thrilling, Eddy? To think that we know an actual Olympic horse and rider!"

Eddy shrugged. He seemed even shier than Drew. He hadn't said much to Lisa, despite her repeated attempts at conversation. Of course, Lisa doubted whether she'd have had much to say to a boy who'd run away from her for a week.

"I guess so," Eddy said, then added to Nigel, "I mean, I think it's great, but, you know—nothing's certain."

"That's right," Nigel said heartily, "nothing's certain. It never is. If Southwood and I do make the team," he added, suddenly serious, "we'll owe it to three young girls we know who call themselves The Saddle Club."

Stevie, Carole, and Lisa blushed with pleasure. "Oh, no," Carole protested, "you'll owe it to Southwood, maybe, and yourself, but not us. We didn't do anything. We wanted to, but we didn't know how."

"Okay," Nigel said agreeably. "I owe it to Southwood, and he owes it to The Saddle Club. You three found Prospero, and seeing Prospero is what convinced me to give Southwood a chance. And you were right, all of you." Nigel looked around the room, but especially at Dorothy. "He could do it. He was ready. A true gold medal horse."

"Then you owe it to Prospero, not us," Lisa said. "I mean, it's not like we went out looking for him. We would have helped any horse that ran across our path."

"For which I am deeply grateful," Drew cut in. His smile rivaled Nigel's. "You can't know how much having him back means to me."

Their food arrived and they all began to eat. "I bet you

remember Prospero when he was at his best, Eddy," Lisa said brightly, around a mouthful of steak. "What was he like then?"

Eddy shrugged. "You've heard Drew talk about him," he said.

Lisa sighed. No matter how many times she tried—and she'd tried a lot this evening—Eddy didn't seem interested in talking to her or to the rest of The Saddle Club. She couldn't blame him. The Dready Eddy Game had been amusing, but it had cost them a chance to get to know someone nice.

12

THE SADDLE CLUB stood at the edge of the crowd, wiggling with excitement. "Here he comes!" They watched as Nigel led Southwood down the pavement at a brisk trot. It was early Sunday morning, the final horse inspection. Southwood stepped out proudly, as though the rigors of the day before had not bothered him at all.

Carole paid particular attention to the way Southwood's feet hit the pavement—even and rhythmic, without a hitch or bobble that might indicate some kind of lameness. If Southwood had injured himself even slightly on cross-country, it would show up when he trotted on a hard surface. Southwood was fine.

He looked fine, too. Nigel and Drew had been up very early, walking Southwood and making sure his muscles hadn't stiffened overnight. They'd groomed him and braided his mane and tail, then polished his dark hooves so that they shone like glass. Nigel was wearing a sport coat and tie, nice trousers, and flashy sunglasses that made Carole giggle. He looked more like a movie star than a champion rider.

Southwood stood for a quick going-over by the show veterinarian, and then Nigel took him back to the stables to prepare for show jumping. Dorothy and Drew went with him. The Saddle Club didn't know where Eddy was—which didn't surprise them, when they thought about it.

"Even after show jumping starts, we'll have to wait a long time to see Southwood," Lisa said, consulting the time sheet they'd gotten at the gate that morning. "The horses jump in reverse order of standings, so Southwood will be one of the last to go."

"Meaning," Stevie said, "that he's near the top!" They all grinned. They knew it didn't really matter what place Southwood ended up getting. As long as he did well, he would have a very good chance of making the British Olympic team.

"What should we do?" Carole asked. "Stevie, do you want another candied apple?"

Stevie put her hand to her stomach and groaned. "After the two I ate yesterday?" she asked. "No thank you! Besides, it's still morning. We just had breakfast."

"Let's have a Saddle Club meeting," Lisa suggested.

They found a spot on a hill overlooking the show-jumping arena. Competition had already started for one of the other divisions, and the girls watched a bay horse bring rails down like rain. They thought of Southwood.

"Never a rail down in competition," Carole murmured, "not one!" They all smiled.

"What was it Nigel called him last night?" Stevie asked. "'A true gold medal horse'? That sounds right. Our Southwood. You're so lucky, Carole. You got to ride him once."

"A long time ago. I'll never forget." Carole's eyes were shining.

"And to think that we might have helped him get to the Olympics," Lisa said. "This trip has been like a dream."

"And to think that tomorrow we'll all be back in Willow Creek, getting ready for school," Stevie added. "That's like a nightmare. This has been the shortest spring break of my life."

"It's been the best one of my life," Lisa said. She paused and bit her lip as she watched a little chestnut horse attack the jumping course with enthusiasm. She let her breath out when the horse went clear. "I'm glad we got to come here, whether we really helped Nigel or not. Just think, we got to see a great horse at the start of his international career. We got to see Nigel accomplish a really spectacular piece of riding over that cross-country course. We got to spend a whole week around some of the best riders and horses in the whole country. Think of all we've learned!"

Stevie laughed. "It's just like you to think in terms of learning, Miss Straight-A Student," she joked.

Lisa threw a clump of grass at her friend. "You know I'm right."

"Oh, I know you are," Stevie said, ducking the grass. "After watching so many horses in the dressage ring, I feel like I really learned how to tell a good dressage test from a bad one. I learned what a great test looks like. That alone made it a great week."

Carole and Lisa grinned. Neither of them shared Stevie's passion for dressage. They'd enjoyed the dressage tests, but they hadn't watched them with Stevie's rapturous intensity.

"I'm a little bit sorry that we didn't give Dready Eddy more of a chance—," Stevie continued.

"More of a chance!" Lisa cut in indignantly. "We didn't give him any chance at all! And now he won't speak to us!" Lisa felt remorseful every time she thought of Eddy's wonderful deep blue eyes.

"—but," Stevie continued, "you know, just because he's good-looking doesn't mean he's nice or fun to be around. Boys are like horses. What you see isn't always the whole story."

Lisa laughed. "I don't think he was impressed by my chicken-pox marks," she said. "Maybe he doesn't know that girls are like horses, too."

"Oh, Lisa, you can hardly see those spots anymore."

"Well," said Lisa, "Eddy doesn't seem to be giving me much of a chance."

"On the other hand," Carole observed, "he's not running away from us."

They all laughed. "It was pretty funny," Lisa said. "Like a reverse scavenger hunt, sort of. If he weren't quite so good-looking, I wouldn't regret it at all!"

"I don't think we spoiled his fun, either," Stevie said. "Drew told me it was really great to spend so much time with his brother, and last night Eddy told Nigel how much he'd enjoyed learning about horses."

"That's good," Carole said.

"If only his eyes weren't quite so blue!" Lisa added. They all laughed again.

"I think we really did help Nigel," Carole said. "He

said so, after all. I think seeing Prospero gave Nigel a sort of outside perspective on his riding—and you know how much that can help. And no matter what, I know we helped Prospero." Carole dug her heels into the grass. "Reuniting him with Drew was one of the luckiest and most satisfying things The Saddle Club has ever done."

"Let's go watch Southwood jump," Stevie said.

AS THEY APPROACHED the ring they saw Dorothy waving them over excitedly. "The British *chef d'équipe*—that's like the coach of the Olympic team—just called from England," she said. "He told Nigel that the team won't be finalized until June, but that if Southwood places in the top ten here, he'll definitely be on the short list."

"Wow!" Carole said, her eyes gleaming. "Does that mean Southwood will be a finalist for the team?"

"Yep," confirmed Dorothy. "There will be ten horses on the short list, and they'll pick the six Olympic horses from those ten."

"Southwood's never had a show-jumping rail down in competition," Lisa recalled. "Not one!"

Dorothy's eyes glittered with excitement. "He could have one down now and still make it," she said. "But only one."

Southwood and Nigel entered the ring.

"I can hardly stand to watch," Stevie whispered. Lisa

pinched her to make her be quiet. Nigel cued Southwood into a canter, and they approached the first fence. Calmly, carefully, Southwood jumped it.

"He makes it look easy," Lisa marveled. Carole nodded. She felt too excited to speak. Southwood continued around the course, jumping in perfect form. As he landed cleanly after the final fence, Nigel's face broke into the biggest grin any of them had ever seen. Dorothy screamed in delight and flung her arms around The Saddle Club, and Southwood galloped across the finish to the sound of their cheers.

"I know I've said this before," Lisa said as they raced to congratulate Nigel, "but I really think this was the best Saddle Club project ever!"

ABOUT THE AUTHOR

BONNIE BRYANT is the author of many books for young readers, including novelizations of movie hits such as *Teenage Mutant Ninja Turtles* and *Honey, I Blew Up the Kid*, written under her married name, B. B. Hiller.

Ms. Bryant began writing The Saddle Club in 1986. Although she had done some riding before that, she intensified her studies then and found herself learning right along with her characters Stevie, Carole, and Lisa. She claims that they are all much better riders than she is.

Ms. Bryant was born and raised in New York City. She still lives there, in Greenwich Village, with her two sons.

GOLD MEDAL HORSES

by

Kimberly Brubaker Bradley

Patrona

NOT ALL HORSES with gold medal spirits win gold medals. Patrona, a dark brown Thoroughbred mare, and her rider, Jil Walton, surprised riders all across America when they were named to the 1992 Olympic three-day event team. Patrona was young, inexperienced, and not well known. Jil was not well known, either. Some people thought it was a mistake to put them on the Olympic team. Some even thought they would not be able to make all the jumps on cross-country day.

But Patrona and Jil surprised everyone again. They jumped in fantastic form and finished first among the Americans. They ended up in seventeenth place—but to them that was as good as gold.

Jil Walton grew up in Walnut, California. Her family

raised horses. They got Patrona as a yearling, and Jil trained her. She did not think Patrona would end up an Olympian—in fact, for several years she tried to sell Patrona.

When Patrona was three, Jil sent her to a barn where hunters were for sale. No one wanted to buy her, so Jil took the mare back and began training her for lower-level events. Patrona did well, but she never seemed like a superstar horse, and Jil kept trying to sell her.

"She surprised me all along," Jil said. "Every time I took her to a higher level of eventing, I'd think it was as high as she could go. When I first rode her at Preliminary, I thought, *This is it. This is where she'll top out.* Then she won. So I took her to Intermediate, and I thought, *No, this is where she'll top out.*"

At every level of eventing, the jumps get higher and more difficult. When Patrona started out, over little fences, she jumped just high enough to clear them. When she moved on to bigger fences, she jumped just high enough to clear those. No matter how big the fences got, Patrona could jump them. But Jil didn't figure this out for a long time.

"I tried to sell her to everyone in the whole state of California," Jil said. Patrona was still for sale when she turned seven, and Jil applied for permission to ride the mare at the advanced level in the spring of 1992. A horse must be at least seven to ride at the advanced level or in the Olympics.

"The committee said, 'Well, you can do a horse trials, but not a three-day event,'" Jil recalled. "Then we won the first advanced horse trials that we entered, and the committee said, 'Okay, you can do a three-day.'"

After Patrona won at the advanced level, Jil decided not to sell her. She began to dream, just a little, about the Olympics.

"At that first advanced horse trials, she just dealt with everything that came her way," Jil said of Patrona. "So I started thinking, *Maybe she can go that far*. But I was thinking about the Atlanta Olympics, and the 1994 World Championships, not about Barcelona." Jil thought the Barcelona Olympics were coming up too soon. She did not think Patrona could be ready.

After competing in two advanced horse trials in early spring, Jil entered Patrona in the 1992 Kentucky Rolex Three-Day Event, the hardest event in North America. Jil also competed a horse named Fax; she and Fax had won a medal at the 1991 Pan American Games. "I thought Fax was going to be the champion," Jil said. "Patrona was so green that I thought, *I'll just jump the first twelve fences and see how it goes*." If Patrona had started out badly or seemed frightened, Jil would have quit, but Patrona did so well that Jil kept going. In the end they

Jil Walton never thought Patrona would make it to the Olympics, but the gallant horse surprised her and everyone else. Here's Jil astride another horse, Tytan. (Shannon Sollinger photo courtesy of *The Chronicle of the Horse*.)

finished third—and they were invited to try out for the Olympic team.

Jil found the Olympic team selection process thrilling. Along with eleven other top-ranked Americans, she took her horse to England for two months of intensive training. Jil loved getting the chance to learn in the company of famous riders she'd admired for her entire life. She also loved showing them what she and Patrona could do.

"On the first day in England, they had us jog the horses up," Jil said. "And the coach said, 'This mare's seven years old?' and I said, 'Yeah.' He said, 'And you plan on riding her around an *Olympic* course?' and I said, 'Yeah!'

"It was like a dare—you put me and that mare in that situation, and we had to prove ourselves." Patrona and Jil made the Olympic team on Jil's twenty-sixth birthday.

Jil says Patrona's attitude, more than anything else, made her an Olympian. "A lot of horses that succeed in eventing are kind of nutty, but Patrona's not. She's incredibly laid-back—very aware, but not in a nervous way. She always has the whole situation sized up in one glance. She's always in control.

"She's like a little schoolteacher who sits there quietly, noticing everything, and then goes off into a phone booth and turns into Wonder Woman.

"And she's incredibly hardheaded. She keeps running

even when she's tired. During the Olympics, she threw a shoe on the steeplechase. We nailed it back on before cross-country, and she just did great. I think she knows that this is her job, and she does it."

Their seventeenth-place finish in the Olympic Games in Barcelona was the highest American placing, but Jil knows they probably could have done better. The cross-country course was incredibly long. Riders could choose to take lower jumps that took longer to get to, or higher jumps on more direct routes. Jil was the second American to go. Since her teammate Mike Plumb had already encountered trouble on the course, Jil's coach told her to take Patrona through the slow routes.

"I had to have a clean round," she explained. For the team to receive a score, three of the four American pairs riding in the cross-country event had to complete the course. (In fact, one of the American pairs was eliminated. The other two American pairs finished forty-eighth and fifty-second, and the United States team ended up tenth overall.) Jil had planned to take many of the slow routes anyway, but after talking to her coach, she switched to taking all of them. Patrona jumped flawlessly, but because they went so slowly they finished with forty-four time penalties.

Here's how Jil described their Olympic cross-country round: "I was really nervous because of Patrona losing that shoe. When you start worrying about things, your horse will pick up on it, so I tried to keep myself calm.

"You couldn't go very fast, because it was so hot. Over the fifth fence, a big ditch-brush, she gave me a huge leap. It was a huge fence, and she was like, 'All *right!*' and she flew over it. I accidentally dropped my whip when she landed. I had to get her through three big water complexes with no whip, but she did just fine. We were very well prepared for what we were supposed to do."

Jil was very pleased with Patrona's performance that day, but she wishes they could ride the course again now that they are more experienced. "I would love to ride Patrona over it today and try all the hard, fast options," she said.

Although they won't return to Barcelona, Jil and Patrona hope to return to the Olympics. Patrona is still young. "She doesn't have a mark on her," Jil said proudly. "She's a very bold, brassy horse"—a true Olympian.

For The Moment

Patrona was one of the youngest horses to ride in the Olympic Games. With her in Barcelona was one of the oldest horses ever to make an Olympic team: the show jumper For The Moment, owned and ridden by American Lisa Jacquin.

Like Jil Walton, Lisa didn't realize at first that her horse might become a superstar. When she bought him he was a six-year-old ex-racehorse. Lisa planned to teach him to jump and then resell him. She named him For The Moment because that was how long she planned to keep him.

"We knew he had the athletic ability to be a great horse," Lisa said. "His biggest problem was that he was difficult in his mind. He didn't want to be disciplined enough to be ridable."

Within two or three years, however, For The Moment was listening to Lisa well enough that she could steer him through the tricky, tight turns on a show-jumping course. At that point she began to realize just how good he was.

"There are a lot of good horses," Lisa said, "but not a lot that want to be great. Like people, some horses don't push themselves hard enough to do their best. Great horses have to have a little bit more fire." For The Moment has plenty of fire.

The big bay Thoroughbred first made the Olympic team in 1988 and helped the United States win the team silver medal in Seoul. In Barcelona the United States placed fifth in show jumping.

At age nineteen, in the 1992 games, For The Moment was considered extremely old for an Olympic horse. What about when he's twenty-three? For The Moment is still healthy and still competing at the highest levels. "He's as good as ever," Lisa said. These days she saves him for big events and plans his schedule carefully so that he doesn't get tired. But if he's ready to try out for the 1996 games in Atlanta, Lisa will let him. For The Moment just might become the only three-time American Olympic horse.

Snowbound

Two other American show jumpers besides For The Moment have competed in two Olympic Games. The first, a brilliant horse named Snowbound, was also the first horse from the United States to win an individual gold medal.

Like For The Moment, Snowbound was an ex-racehorse. While at the racetrack he injured the tendons in his legs, and during his whole show-jumping career these injuries affected him. He did not compete often, but when he did he usually won. His rider, William Steinkraus, said he had "the heart of a lion and the agility of a cat." Snowbound won his gold in 1968. In 1972 he again made the Olympic team but did poorly because his legs were hurting him again. After that Olympics he was retired to a farm in Ireland.

Touch of Class and Abdullah

Touch of Class and Abdullah made history in the individual show-jumping competition in the 1984 Olympics. Touch of Class, a tiny bay Thoroughbred mare, was ridden by an American named Joe Fargis. Abdullah, a big gray German-bred Trakehner stallion, was ridden by Joe Fargis's friend and business partner, Conrad Homfeld.

Olympic show-jumping competition takes place over several days, and the horses jump several rounds. Abdullah was outstanding, but Touch of Class was a bit better. The mare knocked down only one fence in four days of competition. She won the individual gold medal, and Abdullah, close on her heels, won the silver. The United States won the team gold medal as well.

Halla

Halla was a fairy-tale mare who made Hans Gunter-Winkler's dream come true. Hans Gunter-Winkler was a famous German show jumper who rode on six Olympic teams and won seven medals, five of them gold. Halla was a difficult, sensitive mare. Many German riders tried her and thought she was too hard to ride, but Hans liked her. He rode her in his first Olympics in 1956.

As always, the top three scores from the four riders on a

team counted toward the team score. The Germans were doing very well, but one of their horses became ill and had to be removed from the competition. This meant that the other three had to finish the course.

Halla was jumping brilliantly. With one round to go, she was in first place, and so was the German team. But as she landed after the final fence, she tripped and nearly fell. Hans Gunter-Winkler managed to stay on (if he'd fallen, they would have been eliminated), but he injured his stomach muscles severely. He had to ride the final round only a few hours later.

Hans's teammates had to lift him into his saddle. He could barely hold on. Halla was so hard to ride that no one thought she would jump a single fence. Hans couldn't tell her what to do—and surely she would never do it on her own.

But she did. Halla jumped a perfect round with Hans clinging to her back, and together they won the individual gold medal and the team gold medal for Germany.

Charisma

Charisma was another late-blooming horse, but he went on to become one of the greatest three-day event champions of all time. New Zealand rider Mark Todd found Charisma at a small stable in New Zealand. At the time Charisma was named Podge. He was small and plain. He had never done anything spectacular, and no one expected that he ever would. When Mark first saw him, he thought Podge looked like "a fat, hairy pony." Mark gave Podge a try only because he had driven a long way to see him. Once in the saddle, however, Mark liked the horse's movement and attitude. He bought him and renamed him Charisma.

At age thirteen Charisma won the individual three-day event gold medal at the Olympics in Los Angeles. Mark was a dairy farmer, and he had sold most of his herd to pay for his trip to the Olympics. Charisma's gold made it all worthwhile.

In 1988 Charisma, now seventeen, qualified for the Olympics in Seoul. Eventing is such a difficult sport that most horses don't compete at the top for very long— seventeen-year-old Charisma was like a fifty-year-old basketball star! At each phase of the event Mark promised his little horse, "This is your last dressage test. . . . This is your last trip cross-country."

Charisma won the individual gold again. When the three medal winners rode up to the platform, little Charisma was by far the shortest horse. Then the riders dismounted—and Mark Todd was by far the tallest rider! They looked mismatched, but everyone knew by then

132

that they were a perfect pair. True to his promise, Mark retired Charisma immediately after the games.

Stroller

Stroller was not a great horse. He was a great pony. When British rider Marion Coakes was a young girl, she competed him in pony jumper classes. Stroller was a truly brilliant jumper. When Marion turned eighteen and had to move on to adult classes, her parents wanted her to get a full-sized horse. Stroller was only fifty-eight inches tall at the shoulder—most jumpers are sixty-six inches tall or taller, and the jumps themselves are often five feet tall. No pony had ever done well in open—adult—jumping. But Marion believed Stroller would, and she wanted to keep him.

She turned out to be right: Tiny Stroller flew over fences that were higher than his head. Not only did he make the Olympic show-jumping team in 1968, he won the individual silver medal! Stroller was dynamite—a pony, but, like the others, a true gold medal horse.

The author gratefully acknowledges the help of many people, including Cynthia Foley, editor of *J. Michael Plumb's Horse Journal*; L. A. Pomeroy, who handles public relations for the United States Equestrian Team; John Strassburger, publisher of *The Chronicle of the Horse*; and Olympic riders Bruce Davidson, Lendon Gray, Lisa Jacquin, Carol Lavell, William Steinkraus, and Jil Walton.

Did you read Bonnie Bryant's exciting companion novel to GOLD MEDAL HORSE? It's in bookstores now!

With bonus pages about real gold medal riders!

GOLD MEDAL RIDER
The Saddle Club #54

The Saddle Club is thrilled to be attending an international riding competition, even if it means they have to serve as humble grooms for Beatrice Benner and her horse, Southwood. Beatrice is the most spoiled rich girl they've ever met, but she is a talented rider. Then an accident threatens to end her career. Stevie, Carole, and Lisa want their friend Kate Devine to take over, but does Kate have what it takes to be a gold medal rider?

And don't miss the next exciting Saddle Club adventure . . .

CUTTING HORSE
The Saddle Club #56

Handsome teen actor Skye Ransom is on location out West at the Bar None Ranch. He needs The Saddle Club's help. Skye has to ride a cutting and roping horse, but the Hollywood-style steed he's been given doesn't know a cow from a camera. Then the girls get a brilliant idea. They must enlist the help of their friend John Brightstar, who works at the ranch. Unfortunately, the California movie crew is making John's job impossible. The last thing he wants to do is help! It looks as if the girls are in a fix that will have the movie director looking their way and shouting, "Cut!"